OXFORD

RAMEAU

AND

FIRST SATIRE

DENIS DIDEROT (1713–1784) was born at Langres in Champagne, the son of a master cutler who wanted him to follow a career in the Church. He attended the best Paris schools, took a degree in theology in 1735 but turned away from religion and tried his hand briefly at law before deciding to make his way as a translator and writer. In 1746, he was invited to provide a French version of Ephraim Chambers's *Cyclopaedia* (1728). The project became the *Encyclopaedia* (*Encyclopédie*, 1751–72), intended to be a compendium of human knowledge in all fields but also the embodiment of the new 'philosophic' spirit of intellectual enquiry. As editor-in-chief, Diderot became the impresario of the French Enlightenment. But ideas were dangerous, and in 1749 Diderot was imprisoned for four months for publishing opinions judged contrary to religion and the public good. He became a star of the salons, where he was known as a brilliant conversationalist. He invented art criticism, and devised a new form of theatre which would determine the shape of European drama. But in private he pursued ideas of startling orginality in texts like *Supplement to Bougainville's Voyage* (*Supplément au Voyage de Bougainville*) and *D'Alembert's Dream* (*Le Rêve de d'Alembert*), which for the most part were not published until after his death. He anticipated DNA, Darwin, and modern genetics, but also discussed the human and ethical implications of biological materialism in fictions—*The Nun* (*La Religieuse*), *Rameau's Nephew* (*Le Neveu de Rameau*), and *Jacques the Fatalist* (*Jacques le fataliste*)—which seem more at home in our century than in his. His life, spent among books, was uneventful and he rarely strayed far from Paris. In 1773, though, he travelled to St Petersburg to meet his patron, Catherine II. But his hopes of persuading her to implement his 'philosophic' ideas failed, and in 1774 he returned to Paris where he continued talking and writing until his death in 1784.

MARGARET MAULDON has worked as a translator since 1987. For Oxford World's Classics she has translated Zola's *L'Assommoir*, Stendhal's *The Charterhouse of Parma*, Maupassant's *Bel-Ami*, Constant's *Adolphe*, Huysmans's *Against Nature* (winner of the Scott Moncrieff prize for translation, 1999), and Flaubert's *Madame Bovary*.

NICHOLAS CRONK is Director of the Voltaire Foundation and General Editor of *The Complete Works of Voltaire*, and Fellow of St Edmund Hall, Oxford. For Oxford World's Classics he has edited Voltaire's *Letters concerning the English Nation* and Rostand's *Cyrano de Bergerac*.

OXFORD WORLD'S CLASSICS

*For over 100 years Oxford World's Classics have brought
readers closer to the world's great literature. Now with over 700
titles—from the 4,000-year-old myths of Mesopotamia to the
twentieth century's greatest novels—the series makes available
lesser-known as well as celebrated writing.*

*The pocket-sized hardbacks of the early years contained
introductions by Virginia Woolf, T. S. Eliot, Graham Greene,
and other literary figures which enriched the experience of reading.
Today the series is recognized for its fine scholarship and
reliability in texts that span world literature, drama and poetry,
religion, philosophy and politics. Each edition includes perceptive
commentary and essential background information to meet the
changing needs of readers.*

OXFORD WORLD'S CLASSICS

DENIS DIDEROT

Rameau's Nephew
and
First Satire

Translated by
MARGARET MAULDON

With an Introduction and Notes by
NICHOLAS CRONK

OXFORD
UNIVERSITY PRESS

OXFORD

UNIVERSITY PRESS

Great Clarendon Street, Oxford OX2 6DP

Oxford University Press is a department of the University of Oxford.
It furthers the University's objective of excellence in research, scholarship,
and education by publishing worldwide in

Oxford New York

Auckland Cape Town Dar es Salaam Hong Kong Karachi
Kuala Lumpur Madrid Melbourne Mexico City Nairobi
New Delhi Shanghai Taipei Toronto

With offices in

Argentina Austria Brazil Chile Czech Republic France Greece
Guatemala Hungary Italy Japan Poland Portugal Singapore
South Korea Switzerland Thailand Turkey Ukraine Vietnam

Oxford is a registered trade mark of Oxford University Press
in the UK and in certain other countries

Published in the United States
by Oxford University Press Inc., New York

British Library Cataloguing in Publication Data

Data available

Library of Congress Cataloging in Publication Data

Diderot, Denis, 1713–1784.
[Neveu de Rameau. English]
Rameau's nephew ; and, First satire / Denis Diderot ; translated by Margaret Mauldon ;
with an introduction and notes by Nicholas Cronk.
p. cm. — (Oxford world's classics)
Includes bibliographical references.
I. Mauldon, Margaret. II. Cronk, Nicholas. III. Diderot, Denis, 1713–1784.
Satire première. English. IV. Title. V. Title: First satire. VI. Series: Oxford world's
classics (Oxford University Press)
PQ1979.A66E5 2006 848.5′08—dc22 2006011792

Typeset in Ehrhardt
by RefineCatch Limited, Bungay, Suffolk
Printed in Great Britain by
Clays Ltd., St Ives plc

ISBN 0–19–280591–6 978–0–19–280591–1

1

CONTENTS

INTRODUCTION

Man is said to be a Sociable Animal

(ADDISON)

Rameau's Nephew—in French, *Le Neveu de Rameau*—is a work of dazzling paradox, an exploration of the contradictions and complexities of man as 'sociable animal' which is in every way unique. It is arguably the greatest work of the French Enlightenment's greatest writer; yet it was unknown in the century in which it was written. Not one of Denis Diderot's contemporaries mentions the text, and Diderot himself makes no clear reference to it in his private correspondence. Everything about the book—When was it written? Who was it written for? What is it about?—remains tantalizingly uncertain. Even its publication is uniquely odd.

When Diderot died, the manuscript of this unpublished work passed with his other manuscripts to his daughter Mme de Vandeul and her husband; Diderot's prudish son-in-law was apparently shocked by many of these works, and piously bowdlerized those in his care. Luckily, another set of manuscripts had been carefully copied for Catherine the Great, who, in an act of great enlightenment, had bought Diderot's books and papers in 1765 in exchange for a pension paid during his lifetime. An autograph manuscript of *Rameau's Nephew* was therefore sent to St Petersburg after Diderot's death in 1784, and some years later it fell into the hands of Klinger, a German dramatist and officer then posted in Russia. Through him, the document found its way back to Germany and to Schiller, who in turn showed it to Goethe; the latter was enchanted by the work and immediately set to translating it. And so it came about that this work of Diderot's first appeared in print in 1805 in Leipzig, as *Rameaus Neffe*, Goethe accompanying his translation with an extended commentary on the text (extracts from this commentary will be found in the Appendix). Then in 1821 the French version of the text was published for the first time, in Paris. Except that it was not Diderot's text at all, but a fraudulent retranslation back into French of Goethe's German version (with some obscenities added for good measure). This stimulated the publication of another edition in 1823, the so-called Brière edition. This was based on the corrupted Vandeul manuscript (with the obscenities removed), and so was equally inauthentic. Other editions followed in the course of the nineteenth century, all based on manuscripts of dubious provenance. Then, one day in 1890, Georges Monval, the librarian of the Comédie-Française, was visiting the *bouquinistes* on the Quai de Voltaire along the Seine and came across a manuscript with the title 'Second Satire' which he recognized as an autograph of *Le Neveu de Rameau*. He bought it, and the following year published what is the first reliable edition of the text. The manuscript which he discovered, after its long European travels, has today come to rest in the Pierpont Morgan Library in New York. This is a story, then, of a French book first published in German, because a French manuscript sent from Paris to St Petersburg found its way to Germany before travelling to Paris and ending up in New York: it is a fiction worthy of Borges, or of Diderot.

To begin with, when did Diderot write *Rameau's Nephew*? Since there are no references to the work in Diderot's lifetime, we are thrown back on the internal evidence of the text itself, which is of course crowded with specific incidents and anecdotes. Many of these are datable with some precision, though here too the work continues to baffle us. Its overall satirical thrust is aimed at the enemies of Diderot and his fellow encyclopedists who were active in the early 1760s, and one whole group of references—the liaison between Bertin and Mlle Hus, for example, or the allusion to the Opéra in the Rue Saint-Honoré, which burned down in 1763—all point to a date for the action somewhere between 1760 and 1762. But many other allusions belong to a later date: the reference to Voltaire's defence of Maupeou, for example, is to an event of 1771; a reference to Sabatier's *Three Centuries* to a work of 1772. All we can say with certainty is that there is no clear allusion to any incident before 1760, and none to any later than 1774. The chronological references are, moreover, inconsistent. The celebrated composer Jean-Philippe Rameau, uncle of 'Him', died in Paris in 1764: at one point in the text he is referred to as having already died, at another point as being alive. A mistake on the part of Diderot? Perhaps. Or perhaps a deliberate inconsistency designed to jolt the reader into realizing that all is not what it seems.

There are broadly two views about how and when the text was written. Jean Fabre, the scholar who produced the first modern scholarly edition of this work in 1950, dates its beginnings to around 1761, and considers that Diderot went on adding to it over the years until it reached its final form around 1774. More recently, Henri Coulet has argued against this view, suggesting that the dialogue was composed in one creative burst around 1773. He maintains that the organized structure of the book precludes the possibility of its having been composed piecemeal over an extended period, and argues that the multiplicity of allusions to events in the early 1760s are part of a self-consciously nostalgic attempt to re-create in the 1770s the atmosphere of the earlier period. These arguments about genesis are important insofar as they provide clues for the interpretation of this baffling work.

In the first place, what is at issue here is a view of the work's 'unity'. It was long fashionable to speak of a disorderly and chaotic text, a reflection, so the argument ran, of Diderot's own expansive and exuberant personality. He was famously a great talker (as Boswell, among others, noted), and so it seemed natural that he should have created a work featuring two great talkers. For critics to argue in this way seems to suggest a need to excuse what is seen as the incoherence and muddle of the work, and it is also to succumb to a nineteenth-century stereotype of Diderot as a confused and flawed thinker. Coulet's bold assertion that this is a coherent and artfully crafted work challenges us to read it afresh.

Secondly, the arguments about chronology help us to identify the events which stimulated Diderot to write this work, and to place it in his career. Diderot arrived in Paris as a young man to pursue his studies, and began to earn a living by translating books from English. His first original piece of writing was a small, anonymous work entitled *Philosophical Thoughts* (*Pensées philoso-phiques*), in which he attacked the Christian critique of passion, and hinted darkly at atheism and materialism. The work predict-ably aroused a furore, and three years later another controversial work, his *Letter on the Blind* (*Lettre sur les aveugles*), led to his imprisonment at Vincennes for four months. Thereafter he was preoccupied for many years with the editing of the *Encyclopedia* (*Encyclopédie*), and throughout that period he was obliged to struggle with the authorities to keep the project alive. Voltaire, from the safe distance of Ferney, near Geneva, advised Diderot to leave Paris, but he stuck it out, publishing the volumes in defiance of the threat of censorship and the risk of further imprisonment.

The royal road to literary respectability in eighteenth-century France was through the theatre, and Diderot's first play, *The Natural Son* (*Le Fils naturel*), performed in 1757, landed him in hot water: first Jean-Jacques Rousseau took public offence at a line in the play that he felt was critical of him and ended their friendship, then Diderot found himself accused of having plagiar-ized the Italian dramatist Goldoni. Prominent among his critics was Charles Palissot, and worse was to come in 1760 when Palissot parodied all the philosophes and encyclopedists in his play *The Philosophes* (*Les Philosophes*), which enjoyed a noisy success at the Comédie-Française. Diderot was singled out in this play for heavy-handed satirical treatment, but, given the delicacy of his situation regarding the *Encyclopédie*, he was effectively powerless to reply. The ever-present danger of censorship meant that Diderot had to lead a double literary life, with the result that at the time of his death, in 1784, he was remembered first and foremost as the editor of the *Encyclopédie*. Many of his other works, those which today we regard as his masterpieces—*Jacques the Fatalist* (*Jacques le fataliste*), *The Nun* (*La Religieuse*), his art criticism—had been 'published' only in a limited number of manuscript copies in the *Correspondance littéraire*, and remained therefore unknown to a wider reading public until the nineteenth century. (The *Correspondance littéraire* was a manuscript journal containing cultural and other news, halfway between a private letter and a printed periodical, which was produced fortnightly and circulated exclusively to a limited number of the crowned heads of Europe.) And then there was *Rameau's Nephew*, which was not published in any form whatsoever, but which Diderot carefully copied and preserved for the readers of a future generation.

The work is many things, but at one level it is clearly Diderot's settling of accounts with Palissot, his revenge on those enemies of the *Encyclopédie* who continued to harass him all his working life. Jean Fabre believed that the work was an intimate affair, written by Diderot purely for his own private pleasure. Certainly it is true that the text is crammed with elusive references to people and events, and despite the heroic efforts of editors (in particular Fabre, whose pioneering edition has 334 notes), we will never understand fully all the allusions. But does this matter? The very fact that we cannot grasp every last detail of the gossip powerfully conveys to us the confined atmosphere of the literary underworld that Diderot is describing. But Fabre's view that this is a private work should not encourage us to read it only as some sort of autobiographical or confessional text, concerned simply with Diderot's recollections of the opponents of Enlightenment.

Rameau's Nephew also, more importantly, addresses and questions some of the fundamental values of the Enlightenment. That it does so with such a light touch and so elusively makes its enquiry more, not less, complex. Two men sit in a café and talk; they discuss morals and music, and they tell stories. The whole exchange is deceptively casual, notwithstanding the extraordinary physical outbursts of 'Him' when he finds himself, literally, at a loss for words. At the heart of these seemingly aimless discussions is a preoccupation with man as a creature of society. 'Man is said to be a Sociable Animal . . .': so begins one of Addison's *Spectator* essays (no. 9, 1711). The expression is borrowed from Aristotle's *Politics*, but Addison develops the idea in a way characteristic of his century: '. . . and, as an Instance of it, we may observe, that we take all Occasions and Pretences of forming our selves into those little Nocturnal Assemblies, which are commonly known by the Name of *Clubs*.'[1] We think of the Enlightenment as an era of empirical enquiry, in which long-standing beliefs in science and religion were subjected to rational scrutiny. This emphasis on the triumph of reason over superstition can make the period seem a dry one—that at least was the caricature that would be fostered by the Romantic generation. But beyond this fresh emphasis on the power of reason, the ideas of the Enlightenment give to the men and women of the eighteenth century a reinvigorated sense of what it means to be 'human'. Addison's whimsical excursus on the nature of clubs recognizes an important form of sociability, and sets the tone for much of the rest of the century: works like Adam Ferguson's *Essay on the History of Civil Society* (1767) or Adam Smith's *Inquiry into the Nature and Causes of the Wealth of Nations* (1776) signal the beginnings of study of what we would now call the 'human' sciences, the study of man's social relation-ships with his fellow man (and so, by implication, a shift away from theology, and the study of man's metaphysical relationship with God).

The questions of how we 'act' in society, how we influence and interact with one another, are at the heart of this dialogue. Behind the humour of the music lesson, for example, or the hilarious scene at Bertin's dinner table, lie serious questions about human conduct. Philosophical questions: to what extent are a man's actions materially, even mechanistically, determined? Thus, if the Nephew is reluctant to educate his son, that is because if he is 'destined' to make good, it will happen anyway. In the early 1770s, following the publication in 1770 of D'Holbach's hard-line determinist manifesto *The System of Nature* (*Système de la nature*), Diderot became increasingly concerned (for example, in *Jacques the Fatalist* and the *Refutation of Helvétius*) to argue against hard and simplistic determinism. Ethical questions: what are the moral bases for our actions? If the new empirical spirit of

---

[1] *The Spectator*, ed. D. F. Bond (Oxford: Clarendon Press, 1965), i. 39.

enquiry entitles us to question the assumptions of religious faith, why should we not also question the sense of terms like 'virtue' and 'vice'? And aesthetic questions: is 'genius' the most exalted form of human expression? Or the most disruptive? Diderot in the 1760s and 1770s was concerned to bring together ethical and aesthetic principles: as he famously wrote, 'a beautiful life is like a beautiful concert'. The apparently shapeless form of this dialogue permits Diderot to make and test connections between different ideas which would have been difficult in another genre.

These ideas are aired in exchanges between two speakers, and critics have understandably sought to weigh up the individual contributions of each. Some have argued that 'Me' gradually reveals the inconsistencies of 'Him' 's position, while others have seen 'Him' as the central character. Or one can choose to view the exchange as taking place between the rival tensions of one and the same person (as Hegel famously saw 'Him' as a spirit alienated from itself, in dialectical tension with 'Me'). 'Me', the initial narrator, seems sympathetic to begin with, then gradually grows more complacent; while 'Him', seductive at times, appears at other times frankly objectionable. But even if the two interlocutors do seem to resemble the chess-players sitting alongside them in the café, locked in a struggle of strategic moves, it is not clear that we can or should try to empathize with either, let alone declare a winner. Nor can we judge the arguments on the basis of words and reason alone, for the exchange is not conducted simply at the level of language. The extraordinary scenes in which 'Me' describes the Nephew miming a piece of music, for example, seem to suggest that human language is not sufficient, and that human beings need other channels through which to express themselves. The discussions about music, which could seem irrelevant to the other concerns of the dialogue, are at root an argument about expressivity: between French and Italian music, which most closely mimics the passions? And which therefore is the most moving? At the heart of all the exchanges between 'Me' and 'Him' is a debate about expressivity and performance.

Precisely what sort of book is this? To what literary genre does it belong? Many modern editions, including the most recent Pléiade version (2004), lump this text together with the other works of fiction (and so separate it from the *First Satire*). But this is no novel in any conventional sense of the term, even if Jules Janin, a nineteenth-century journalist, did publish a continuation of the dialogue which tries to assimilate Diderot's form into the conventions of nineteenth-century fiction.[2] We might be tempted to think of the work as a play: it creates drama out of the contrast of two characters, and the action takes place over a defined period in a defined place. The role of the Nephew, with its elements of mime and impersonation, offers great potential to an actor, so it is no surprise that the work was performed on stage in France as early as 1860, and has been frequently staged in recent years, following an enormously successful production in Paris in 1963.[3] But again, this is no play in any conventional sense. Perhaps the best we can do is to fall back on the description of the work as a dialogue: the dialogue was a well-established literary genre in France in the seventeenth and eighteenth centuries, more familiar to Diderot's contemporaries than to us. But *Rameau's Nephew* scarcely resembles these contemporary models (any more than it resembles the classical model of, say, Plato), so if it is a dialogue, it is an innovative dialogue which seemingly owes little to tradition. It is nonetheless instructive to look more closely at how this work distinguishes itself from other works in dialogue form.

A conventional literary dialogue, in the style, say, of Fontenelle, took place between two characters with token names and personalities—in effect, an encounter between two talking heads. Diderot turns this tradition around by creating a dialogue between real people, who are of course not real. 'Me' refers, in some sense, to Diderot, just as 'Him' refers to Jean-François Rameau, the bohemian nephew of the great French composer Jean-Philippe

---

[2] See Jules Janin, *La Fin d'un monde et du Neveu de Rameau*, ed. Joseph-Marc Bailbé (Paris: Klincksieck, 1977).

[3] See *L'Avant-Scène*, 303 (15 Jan. 1964), and the recording described on p. xxx.

Rameau. Yet 'Him' is not of course presented as a real-life portrait of Rameau: to take only the most glaring example, 'Him' in
the dialogue defends the view (which is also Rousseau's) that the
Italian language is more suited to music than French, whereas the
(real) J.-F. Rameau maintained the opposite view. Other real-life
characters, like the Abbé Galiani, have also left their mark on the
character of 'Him'. To maintain, as some critics have done, that
'Him' is a parodic or stylized portrait of Rousseau is misleading
and unhelpful. And for all that the Nephew is an extraordinary
literary creation based on a real person, he is also an example of a
specific contemporary type, the Grub Street hack, memorably
celebrated in Dr Johnson's *Life of Richard Savage* (1744). The
number of books printed, and so the number of individuals who
could style themselves writers, grew enormously in the eighteenth
century, and Robert Darnton has contrasted the High Enlightenment of the philosophes (Voltaire, Diderot, and the like) with the
low life of the scribblers who scraped a living with journalism
or other forms of hack writing.[4] The Nephew thus represents
a specific phenomenon of the contemporary literary scene. Other
writers of the period create such characters—Marivaux's
The Indigent Philosopher (*L'Indigent philosophe*, 1727), Voltaire's
The Poor Devil (*Le Pauvre diable*, 1760)—though none rival the
exuberance of Diderot's creation.

The setting of the dialogue is also interesting. In earlier French
dialogues the exchanges generally took place in a stylized and
closed setting, either outside in an elegant (and conveniently
empty) park, or inside in a study, where there was no chance of
disturbance. In such cases, the abstract sense of place was entirely
fitting for the equally abstract exchange of ideas: the whole intention was to transcend the everyday. Diderot's purpose is radically
different: he sets his dialogue in a café, and not just any café,
but the Café de la Régence, in the Place du Palais-Royal in the
heart of Paris, and a favourite haunt of Diderot himself. The

[4] Robert Darnton, *The Literary Underground of the Old Régime* (Cambridge, Mass.:
Harvard University Press, 1982).

Narrator explains in the opening lines that he likes to walk in the Palais-Royal gardens around five in the afternoon, and that he takes refuge in the café when it is cold or wet. His picture of the chess-players seated in the café describes a reality of mid-eighteenth-century Paris. Then, at the end of the dialogue, 'Him' leaves to attend the Opéra, where performances began in that period at six. The building—it had been Molière's theatre until his death, when it was taken over by Lully—was situated just opposite the Café de la Régence, and reached down a narrow street from the gardens of the Palais-Royal. Thus the entire dialogue is played out in a precisely defined part of the city (now occupied by the Comédie-Française and the Place du Palais-Royal), and to that extent we may say that the setting is 'realistic' in a way unprecedented in a philosophical dialogue.

But what is noteworthy here is not so much the 'realism' of this setting as its rich symbolic significance. Already in the eighteenth century the café was associated with philosophical and literary debate and dispute, for example in Montesquieu's *Persian Letters* (letter 36), and it was no coincidence that the most influential periodical of the Italian Enlightenment, founded by the Verri brothers in 1764, was called *The Café* (*Il Caffè*). Much recent work on the Enlightenment has been inspired by Habermas's notion of public space and his suggestion that Enlightenment discourse was facilitated by the emergence of what he termed the 'bourgeois public sphere'.[5] The café, like the inn or the Masonic lodge, fostered a new form of sociability, and, in conjunction with the newspapers and brochures made possible by the burgeoning print culture, provided forums for the emergence of public opinion. (Public opinion could be said to be an eighteenth-century invention, and it is fitting that the word 'opinion' occurs in this sense in the French text of *Rameau's Nephew*.)

---

[5] Jürgen Habermas, *The Structural Transformation of the Public Sphere*, trans. T. Burger (Cambridge, Mass.: MIT Press, 1989); for a discussion of the notion of the public sphere, see Craig Calhoun (ed.), *Habermas and the Public Sphere* (Cambridge, Mass.: Harvard University Press, 1992).

Thus the drama of *Rameau's Nephew* is played out entirely in
the public urban spaces of mid-eighteenth-century Paris. The
Palais-Royal gardens are an open and public space, where people
go to walk, to think, to meet friends, and, in the Allée de Foy, to
meet prostitutes. It is the very freedom that this space permits
which allows the Narrator to ponder in the opening lines that
'my thoughts are my little flirts'; and later the Nephew recalls
Carmontelle's image of his famous uncle walking, bent over, in
the gardens (p. 17; see frontispiece). The Café de la Régence is
another such public space, as is the Opéra, to which the Nephew
hurries at the end, summoned by the bell. The full significance of
the Nephew's extravagant outbursts can only be understood in
this context of public space; his eccentric behaviour, unthinkable
in a salon, is at least permissible in a café, whose clientèle is more
mixed, and more querulous.

If the Nephew's mad behaviour can be situated in the public
space of the contemporary city, it is also underpinned by a number
of literary models, many of them more familiar to an eighteenth-
century readership than to a modern one. Prime among these is
Erasmus's *Praise of Folly* (1509), which was well known to
Diderot: there were at least half-a-dozen editions in the eighteenth century, and Diderot quotes the work in his *Salon of 1767*.
The Nephew is in one sense a modern reincarnation of Erasmus's
fool, and the theme of folly is central to Diderot's text too: the
word *fou* (mad/madman) occurs twenty-seven times, the word
folie (madness) six times. This archetype of the fool whose role is
to bring forth the truth is not, of course, limited to Erasmus; it is
significant that Diderot cites Rabelais in the text, and he may
have in mind in particular the *Third Book*, in which Pantagruel
reminds Panurge of the proverbial 'A madman teaches a wise
man well.'[6]

Beyond the specific model of the fool, Diderot draws on the
broader tradition of carnivalesque writing. Carnival is the name

---

[6] Rabelais, *Le Tiers Livre*, ch. 37; see also chs. 46 and 47, in which Triboulet plays the
fool in order to show the truth about Panurge's marriage plans.

given to that moment in medieval and Renaissance societies when, for a limited period, the world was turned upside-down, and the pagan could dress as a priest, the beggar as a king; the carnival mask gave temporary festive immunity and allowed everyone to say the unsayable. The Russian critic Mikhail Bakhtin has argued that even as this social phenomenon went into decline after the sixteenth century, 'the carnival spirit and grotesque imagery continued to live and was transmitted as a now purely literary tradition'.[7] In this context, Bakhtin has written in particular about the sixteenth-century writer Rabelais as an exemplar of literary carnival, focusing on his emphasis on different linguistic registers, from obscene to learned, on his banquet imagery, and on his use of the grotesque body. Elements of this carnival culture survive in the eighteenth century, for example, in the fairs held in Paris—some of the theatrical works referred to in the text were performed at these fairs. The Narrator's initial description of the Nephew's 'type' makes clear that he is to be situated in a carnival context:

I hold such eccentrics in low esteem . . . maybe once a year I like to stop and spend time with them, because their character contrasts sharply with other men's, and they break with that tedious uniformity which our education, our social conventions, and our customary proprieties have produced. If one of them appears in a group, he's like a grain of yeast that ferments, and restores to each of us his natural individuality. He shocks us, he stirs us up; he forces us to praise or blame, he brings out the truth . . . (p. 4)

The text will go on to present the Nephew as a true king of Carnival, someone who, for a strictly limited period, is allowed to act without check, the Fool who is allowed to speak the truth; and the very fact that the Narrator likes to spend time with the Nephew 'once a year' seems to point to a calendar of carnival. In the best carnival tradition, this entire text becomes a ceremonious

---

[7] Mikhail Bakhtin, *Rabelais and His World*, trans. H. Iswolsky (Bloomington: Indiana University Press, 1984), 34.

dethroning of philosophy.[8] In this context, another model for Diderot is the second-century Greek satirist Lucian, whose philosophical dialogues include, for example, several on the theme of the poor man in the rich man's house.[9] It is not surprising, therefore, that Bakhtin includes Diderot's philosophical narratives in his history of carnivalesque literature.[10]

The autograph manuscript of *Rameau's Nephew* bears the simple title, in Diderot's hand, *Second Satire*. The further title, 'Rameau's Nephew', is added in another hand, and while one can understand that editors and publishers have always preferred this more racy form (used in every printed edition, from the 1805 German version onwards), there are good reasons for keeping in mind Diderot's title, as expressed in the only authentic manuscript. Not least, the *Second Satire* usefully reminds us of the shorter and less well-known *First Satire*. Written in 1773, the *First Satire* was initially published in 1778, in the limited manuscript circulation of the *Correspondance littéraire* (where it was entitled simply *Satire*); the work was first printed posthumously, in the so-called Naigeon edition of Diderot's works, in 1798, where for the first time it acquired its title *First Satire*.

The question of the relationship of the *First Satire* to the *Second* is a tricky one. If we assume the traditional view that Diderot began *Rameau's Nephew* in the early 1760s, then the title *Second Satire* must represent an addition to the evolving work made after the composition of the *First Satire*. But if we accept Coulet's more recent thesis that *Rameau's Nephew* was composed in one creative spurt around 1773–4, then it becomes entirely possible that he wrote the two *Satires* in numerical order, as it

---

[8] See Huguette Cohen, 'La Tradition gauloise et le carnavalesque dans *Les Bijoux indiscrets*, *Le Neveu de Rameau* et *Jacques le fataliste*', in *Colloque international Diderot*, ed. A.-M. Chouillet (Paris: Aux Amateurs de Livres, 1985), 229–37.

[9] See e.g. Lucian's *The Dependent Scholar*, *The Parasite*, and *Saturnalian Letters*; the same theme is broached in the Latin playwright Terence's *The Eunuch*. Lucian's *Of Pantomime* may also have caught Diderot's attention.

[10] See Nicholas Cronk, '*Jacques le fataliste* et le renouveau du roman carnavalesque', *Dix-Huitième Siècle*, 32 (2000), 33–49.

were, and within a short space of time. In June 1773 Diderot left
Paris to travel to Russia by way of Holland; it was the one great
journey of his life, and he would not return to Paris until October
the following year. On his way to St Petersburg he wrote to his
friend Mme d'Épinay from Holland that he had enjoyed himself
writing 'a small satire' which he had already planned before leaving Paris: this must refer to the *First Satire*. Near the end of the
work he asks Naigeon to remember him to his friends in Paris, so
he is clearly writing from abroad; and he earlier refers to a conversation he had had with the historian and poet Rulhière shortly
before his departure for Russia. This being the case, it is entirely
possible that the *First Satire* was written in Holland in 1773, and
that the *Second Satire* was begun soon thereafter. Those who have
argued for the composition of *Rameau's Nephew* over a prolonged
period have pointed to the date of the various anecdotes, stretching from around 1760 to 1774; in this connection, it is worth
noting that the stories told in the *First Satire* similarly stretch
from 1746 to 1773, and we can be certain in this case that the
work was written in one go. It seems that both works, with their
celebratory frescos of Parisian literary life, were written with the
nostalgia of the exile.

The *First Satire* is cast in the form of a letter addressed by
Diderot to his friend and disciple Jacques-André Naigeon, a
militant atheist, and like the *Second Satire*, it employs dialogue,
with Naigeon seemingly as interlocutor as well as addressee. An
obvious link between the two *Satires* is that they have an over-
lapping cast of characters: Sophie Arnould appears in both
works, as does the Abbé de Canaye. There is a further evident
link in Diderot's interest in what he calls 'the word of character',
that is, the telling phrase or expression which sums up a whole
person. This interest is hardly new, for he had hinted at it twenty
years earlier, in his article 'Encyclopedia' in the *Encyclopédie*
(vol. 5, 1755):

It is important sometimes to mention absurd things, but it must be
done lightly and in passing, simply for the history of the human soul,

which reveals itself better in certain odd incidents than in some eminently reasonable action. These incidents are for moralists what the dissection of a monster is for the natural historian: it is more useful to him than the study of a hundred identical individuals. There are certain words which describe more powerfully and more completely than an entire speech.

Such 'words of character' make up the substantial part of the *First Satire*, and at the same time pave the way for *Rameau's Nephew, Second Satire*, in which they recur as a constituent part of the characterization of 'Him'. Diderot's interest in these forms of expression goes beyond his liking for a good story; they are central to his philosophy of man and to his attempt to bring together ethical, metaphysical, and aesthetic concerns.

When considering Aristotle's 'sociable animal' from the standpoint of the Enlightenment, we tend to focus, naturally enough, on sociability. Such is Montesquieu's emphasis in the *Persian Letters* (letter 87). Diderot, almost uniquely among his contemporaries (but in the best tradition of satire), invites us to focus also on the other side of the coin, that is to say, on animality. The *First Satire* begins with a bravura account of a human bestiary: in the manner of classical satire, all men can be classified by animal types. The overt treatment of this theme here makes us reread the *Second Satire* in a different light, for it is one of the striking characteristics of the Nephew that he uses forceful animal imagery throughout. He likens himself and others to dogs, he is 'cock of the roost' in the Bertin household, and a worm when he is expelled from it; on other occasions he compares himself and his like to wolves and to tigers, while he describes others as monkeys, geese, and so forth. For the Nephew, the world is a jungle, and 'in nature all the species prey on one another; in society all the classes do the same' (p. 31)—this does not sound much like Addison's 'sociable animal'. Addison was taking his cue from Locke, for whom man is by nature social. But Diderot has in mind perhaps an earlier English philosopher, Thomas Hobbes, who held a mechanistic view of life as simply the movements of the organism; since man was a selfishly individualistic animal at constant war with all other men, society could exist only by the power of the state. In the clash between 'Me' and 'Him', Addison's comfortable view of man as sociable animal is exploded as Diderot stages for us the clash between Locke and Hobbes.

These allusions to animals take us to the heart of the satirical tradition. At one point in the *First Satire* the narrator excuses himself for writing almost in the manner of the Roman satirist Persius, whose poems had a hard edge, rather than explaining a passage of Horace, whose milder satire was tinged with epicureanism. Both of Diderot's *Satires* begin with epigraphs from the *Satires* of Horace; and the 'post-scriptum' to the *First Satire*, which is a discussion of certain passages in Horace, seems to be the continuation in print of a debate which Diderot was conducting with his friend Naigeon, a learned Latinist. The epigraph of the *First Satire* is taken from Horace, *Satires*, II. i: the line in question, 'For every thousand living souls, there are as many thousand tastes', straightforwardly sets the tone for what is to follow. But the dedication to Naigeon which comes after, and which quotes the opening lines of the poem, seems to suggest that Diderot is also alluding to the poem as a whole. Horace opens his second book of *Satires* with a reflection on the nature of satire itself; his opening poem is cast in the form of a dialogue between the poet and a famous lawyer. Horace pretends to ask for legal advice about how to write satire, the lawyer unhelpfully advises him to write something safer, like epic (the same advice would have held good for Diderot in the eighteenth century). Horace accepts that it would be illegal to publish libellous verses; and the lawyer accepts that even libellous verses, if they are well written and win Caesar's approval, are safe from prosecution. Horace, secure in his position as a writer, can afford to be ironical, but beneath the surface is a serious discussion about the freedom of speech which a poet can legitimately enjoy; this is a theme which is all too pertinent for Diderot and his fellow philosophes writing in the shadow of the *ancien régime*'s arcane censorship practices.

The epigraph at the beginning of *Rameau's Nephew* is taken
from Horace, *Satires*, II. vii. Again, the specific reference to
Vertumnus, the god who could assume any shape he chose,
alludes to the chameleon personality of the Nephew, and seems
obvious enough. But to readers steeped in Horace's poetry (as all
educated eighteenth-century readers were), it is hard not to think
that Diderot also wants us to bear in mind the poem as a whole.
Satire II. vii is one of two (the other is II. iii) which Horace sets in
Rome during the period of Saturnalia, the annual three-day feast
in commemoration of the golden age of Saturn, when the usual
proprieties were turned upside-down and all men were treated as
equal; thus the very epigraph establishes the theme of carnival.
In Lucian's *Saturnalia*, for example, a poor man writes to the
king asking to be allowed to sup at the table of a rich man during
the period of the festival—a request which anticipates the
Nephew's presence in the Bertin household. Horace's slave
Davus makes use of this temporary state of grace to tell his
master openly about his faults; the satire is again in dialogue
form, and it is the slave here who speaks wisdom as he shows that
the master is no freer than his slave, and who goes on to reveal
mankind's follies.

Diderot's works largely defy easy generic classification, and his
description of these two pieces as satires is untypically precise. In
signalling the generic link to Horace, he gives us vital clues as to
how to read these texts. The term 'satire' means etymologically a
pot-pourri, a mixture of different things, and it is easy—perhaps
too easy—to dismiss the seeming confusion of *Rameau's Nephew*
as nothing more than satire's habitual disorderly mix. In this
spirit, the French critic Taine in the nineteenth century described
Rameau's Nephew as 'an incomparable monster and an immortal
document'. On the one hand, these two satires are works that
satirize the literary world of their day, products of a moment in
the 1760s that was one of the tensest in Louis XV's reign, when
the arguments over the censorship of the *Encyclopédie* were taking
place against the backdrop of the Damiens affair (a bungled and
amateurish attempt to assassinate the King) and the Seven Years

War with England. On the other hand, these literary works are timeless in the way they can be enjoyed even by readers without particular knowledge of the French *ancien régime*. Many of the specific references in Diderot's two *Satires* remain hermetic even now; but it is worth remembering that the same is true of Horace's work. In neither case does this prevent us from admiring their literary achievement. What makes Diderot's satires such seminal Enlightenment texts is that they both express the enlightened values of reason and civility and at the same time question them. In their exploration of the 'sociable animal' they probe, more than other texts of the period, both man's social and animal nature.

Above all, we continue to relish these texts because they repeatedly force us to question our own assumptions, and this must surely explain both their lasting fascination and their continuing influence. The *First Satire* has left a clear trace in the fiction of Balzac.[11] As for the *Second Satire*, it is extraordinary how so many readers, from Goethe and Hegel to Foucault, have been inspired by *Rameau's Nephew*. It is a text which, precisely because of its mystery, seems able to inspire different readers to write wholly different texts. Thomas Bernhard, in *Wittgenstein's Nephew* (*Wittgensteins Neffe*, 1983), uses the model of Diderot's work to provide a framework for an autobiographical narration about his meeting in an asylum with Paul Wittgenstein, grand-nephew of the famous philosopher. Meanwhile Jacques-Alain Miller has recently published a psychoanalytical rewriting of the text (*Le Neveu de Lacan, satire*, 2003). Alberto Moravia's novel *Me and Him* (*Io e lui*, 1971), in which a man dialogues with his penis, may or may not be indebted to Diderot, but there is a clear influence on Saul Bellow's first novel, *Dangling Man* (1944), which describes the isolation of an intellectual in wartime, as he passes the time while waiting to be called up by studying Diderot and other Enlightenment writers: Diderot's dialogue provides a

[11] See Jean Pommier, 'Comment Balzac relaie Diderot', *Revue des Sciences Humaines* (Apr.–Sept. 1951), 161–6.

structural and philosophical model for Bellow's novel, and there
are evident similarities between the hero Joseph and Rameau's
Nephew.[12]

If Diderot's *Satires* continue to fascinate, it is surely because
they continue to amuse as well as disturb us. For one critic,
Rameau's Nephew 'is a moral and aesthetic experiment, one which
disturbs complacency at every moment and leads to no restful
conclusion'.[13] At one point, halfway through the work, 'Me' stops
'Him' and says: 'What do you mean, exactly? Are you being
ironic, or sincere?' (p. 44). 'Him' continues with his paradoxical
defence of wrongdoing, and 'Me' again exclaims: 'I confess that
I can't tell whether what you're saying is sincere or spiteful. I'm a
simple soul: I wish you'd say what you mean to me and not bother
about being clever.' If we feel confused by this, so did Goethe.
On 21 December 1804 he wrote to Schiller: 'This dialogue
explodes like a bomb in the middle of French literature, and it
takes considerable skill to know what precisely is touched by the
fall-out, and how . . .'

[12] See Sanford Pinsker, 'Rameau's Nephew and Saul Bellow's *Dangling Man*', *Notes on Modern American Literature*, 4 (1980), item 22; and Jo Brans, 'The Dialectic of Hero and Anti-Hero in Rameau's Nephew and *Dangling Man*', *Studies in the Novel*, 16: 4 (1984), 435–47.
[13] Lester G. Crocker, *Diderot's Chaotic Order: Approach to Synthesis* (Princeton: Princeton University Press, 1974), 92.

NOTE ON THE TEXT

Rameau's Nephew

This work (*Le Neveu de Rameau*) remained unpublished and unknown in Diderot's lifetime. Various editions appeared in the course of the nineteenth century, all of them based on unreliable manuscripts (see Introduction for details). An autograph manuscript, entitled 'Seconde Satire' ('Second Satire'), was discovered in the late nineteenth century and is now in the Pierpont Morgan Library, New York. This manuscript, edited and published for the first time by Georges Monval in 1891, has provided the base text of all modern editions. It remains the only known autograph manuscript, and the other extant non-autograph manuscripts are probably derived from it. The first translation based on the autograph manuscript was by Sylvia Margaret Bell, published in London by Longmans, Green & Co. in 1897. The present translation is based on the edition by Henri Coulet in *Œuvres complètes*, vol. 12 (Paris: Hermann, 1989), which emends earlier readings of the Pierpont Morgan Library manuscript in some instances.

First Satire

This work (*Satire première*) first appeared in the October 1778 issue of the manuscript journal *Correspondance littéraire*. It was first printed in the Naigeon edition of Diderot's works (1798). The present translation is based on the Coulet edition (see above), which takes as its base text one of the Gotha manuscripts of the *Correspondance littéraire*.

SELECT BIBLIOGRAPHY

Critical Editions

Le Neveu de Rameau

ed. Jean Fabre (Geneva: Droz, 1950): a pioneering edition, with extensive notes, and a useful 'Lexique' to the language of the text.

ed. Roland Desné (Paris: Éditions sociales, 1972).

ed. Jacques Chouillet (Paris: Imprimerie nationale, 1982).

ed. Henri Coulet, in Diderot, *Œuvres complètes* (Paris: Hermann), vol. 12 (1989): the most scrupulous edition of the autograph manuscript; excellent introduction.

ed. Pierre Chartier (Paris: Livre de Poche, 2002): the most complete and up-to-date paperback edition.

ed. Michel Delon, in *Contes et romans*, Bibliothèque de la Pléiade (Paris: Gallimard, 2004).

Satire première

ed. Donal O'Gorman, in *Diderot the Satirist* (Toronto: University of Toronto Press, 1971): based on the Naigeon printed edition.

ed. Roland Desné, in *Le Neveu de Rameau* (Paris, Éditions sociales, 1972).

ed. Henri Coulet, in Diderot, *Œuvres complètes* (Paris: Hermann), vol. 12 (1989): based on one of the Gotha manuscripts of the *Correspondance littéraire*.

ed. Pierre Chartier, in *Le Neveu de Rameau* (Paris: Livre de Poche, 2002): most accessible edition; text based on Coulet edition.

Critical Studies in English

Herbert Dieckmann, 'The Relationship Between Diderot's *Satire I* and *Satire II*', *Romanic Review*, 43 (1952), 12–26.

Hans Robert Jauss, 'The Dialogical and the Dialectical *Neveu de Rameau*: How Diderot Adopted Socrates and Hegel Adopted Diderot', with responses (Berkeley, Cal.: Center for Hermeneutical studies in Hellenistic and Modern Culture, 1983).

Herbert Josephs, *Diderot's Dialogue of Language and Gesture: 'Le Neveu de Rameau'* (Columbus, Ohio: Ohio State University Press, 1969).

Select Bibliography

Apostolos Kouidis, 'The Praise of Folly: Diderot's Model for Le Neveu de Rameau', Studies on Voltaire and the Eighteenth Century, 185 (1980), 237–66.

Donal O'Gorman, Diderot the Satirist (Toronto: University of Toronto Press, 1971).

Walter E. Rex, 'Music and the Unity of Le Neveu de Rameau', Diderot Studies, 29 (2003), 83–99.

Jack Undank, 'On Being "Human": Diderot's Satire première', Eighteenth-century Studies, 20 (1986–7), 1–16.

Critical Studies in French

Jacques Chouillet, 'L'Espace urbain et sa fonction textuelle dans Le Neveu de Rameau', in La Ville au dix-huitième siècle (Aix-en-Provence: Edisud, 1975), 71–81.

Michèle Duchet and Michel Launay, Entretiens sur Le Neveu de Rameau (Paris: Nizet, 1967).

Pierre Hartmann, 'Un si lumineux aveuglement: une étude sur Le Neveu de Rameau et la crise des Lumières', Diderot Studies, 26 (1995), 125–69.

Marian Hobson, 'Pantomime, spasme et parataxe: Le Neveu de Rameau', Revue de métaphysique et de morale, 89 (1984), 197–213.

—— 'Déictique, dialectique dans Le Neveu de Rameau', Cahiers Textuel, 11 (1992), 11–19.

Philip Knee, 'Diderot et Montaigne: morale et scepticisme dans Le Neveu de Rameau', Diderot Studies, 29 (2003), 35–51.

André Magnan (ed.), Rameau le Neveu: textes et documents (Saint-Étienne, 1993).

Roland Mortier and Raymond Trousson (eds.), Dictionnaire de Diderot (Paris: Champion, 1999).

José-Michel Moureaux, 'Le Rôle du fou dans Le Neveu de Rameau', in Le Siècle de Voltaire: hommage à René Pomeau, ed. C. Mervaud and S. Menant (Oxford: Voltaire Foundation, 1987), ii. 675–91.

Stéphane Pujol, 'L'Espace public du Neveu de Rameau', RHLF, 93 (1993), 669–84.

Jean Starobinski, 'Le Dîner chez Bertin', in Das Komische, ed. W. Preisendanz and R. Warning (Munich: W. Fink, 1976), 191–204.

—— 'L'Incipit du Neveu de Rameau', Nouvelle Revue Française, 347 (1 Dec. 1981), 42–64.

Select Bibliography

—— 'Sur l'emploi du chiasme dans *Le Neveu de Rameau*', *Revue de métaphysique et de morale*, 89 (1984), 182–96.

—— 'Diogène dans *Le Neveu de Rameau*', *Stanford French Review*, 8 (1984), 147–65.

Eric Walter, 'Un déplacement stratégique dans le Texte-Diderot', *Littérature*, 29 (Feb. 1978), 105–15.

—— 'Les «intellectuels du ruisseau» et *Le Neveu de Rameau*', *Cahiers Textuel*, 11 (1992), 43–59.

Further Reading

Daniel Brewer, *The Discourse of Enlightenment in Eighteenth-century France: Diderot and the Art of Philosophizing* (Cambridge: Cambridge University Press, 1993).

Robert Darnton, *The Literary Underground of the Old Régime* (Cambridge, Mass.: Harvard University Press, 1982): in particular, the essays 'The High Enlightenment and the low-life of literature in pre-revolutionary France' and 'A pamphleteer on the run'.

Michel Foucault, *Madness and Civilization: A History of Insanity in the Age of Reason*, trans. R. Howard (London: Routledge, 2001).

Peter France, *Diderot* (Oxford: Oxford University Press, 1983).

—— (trans.), *Diderot's Letters to Sophie Volland* (Oxford: Oxford University Press, 1972).

P. N. Furbank, *Diderot: A Critical Biography* (London: Secker & Warburg, 1992).

David Garrioch, *The Making of Revolutionary Paris* (Berkeley: University of California Press, 1972).

Richard Holmes, *Dr Johnson & Mr Savage* (London: Hodder & Stoughton, 1993).

G. W. F. Hegel, *Phenomenology of Spirit*, trans. A. V. Miller, ed. J. N. Findlay (Oxford: Oxford University Press, 1977).

Cynthia Verba, *Music and the French Enlightenment: Reconstruction of a Dialogue 1750–1764* (Oxford: Clarendon Press, 1993).

Arthur M. Wilson, *Diderot* (New York: Oxford University Press, 1972).

Select Bibliography

Film

See Eva Maria Stadler, '*Rameau's Nephew by Diderot* . . . : un film de Michael Snow', in *Interpréter Diderot aujourd'hui*, ed. E. de Fontenay and J. Proust (Paris: Le Sycomore, 1984), 9–116.

Recording in French

CD (Adès 13.259–2), released 1988 (original recording released 1964): extracts from the stage performance given in 1963 at the Théâtre de la Michodière, Paris. 'Lui' is played by Pierre Fresnay, 'Moi' by Julien Bertheau.

Further Reading in Oxford World's Classics

Denis Diderot, *Jacques the Fatalist*, trans. and ed. David Coward.
—— *The Nun*, trans. and ed. Russell Goulbourne.
Lucian, *Selected Dialogues*, trans. and ed. C. D. N. Costa.
Jean-Jacques Rousseau, *Confessions*, trans. Angela Scholar, ed. Patrick Coleman.
Voltaire, *Candide and Other Stories*, trans. and ed. Roger Pearson.
—— *Letters concerning the English Nation*, ed. Nicholas Cronk.

A CHRONOLOGY OF DENIS DIDEROT

1713 5 October: birth of Denis Diderot at Langres, first child of Didier Diderot (1675–1759), a master cutler, and Angélique Vigneron (1677–1748), a tanner's daughter. There followed Denise (1715–97), Catherine (1716–18), Catherine (II) (1719–35), Angélique (1720–48), who took the veil and died mad, and Didier-Pierre (1722–87), a strict churchman who could not tolerate his brother's atheism.

1723 Enters the Jesuit college at Langres.

1726 22 August: receives the tonsure, the first step towards an ecclesiastical career.

1728 Autumn: moves to Paris to continue his education at the Collège Louis-le-Grand, the Jansenist Collège d'Harcourt, and the Collège de Beauvais.

1732 2 September: Master of Arts.

1735 6 August: awarded a bachelor's degree in theology but, after applying unsuccessfully for a living, abandons his plans for a career in the Church and takes up law, with the reluctant approval of his father.

1737 Abandons law and makes a meagre living as a private tutor, translator, and supplier of sermons to the clergy. Frère Ange, at Diderot's father's request, keeps an eye on him.

1741 Contemplates entering the seminary of Saint-Sulpice in Paris, but falls in love with Antoinette Champion (1710–96).

1742 Meets Jean-Jacques Rousseau.

1743 January: His father refuses to allow him to marry Antoinette and has him detained in a monastery at Langres, from which he escapes a month later. 6 November: marries Antoinette secretly in Paris. Publication of his translation of Temple Stanyan's *History of Greece*.

1744 Birth of Angélique, who lives only a few weeks. Meets Condillac and begins following a course of lectures in surgery.

1745 Translates Shaftesbury's *Inquiry concerning Virtue, or Merit*.

1746 Beginning of a liaison with Mme de Puisieux which lasts until
1751. Invited by the publisher Le Breton to translate Ephraim
Chambers's *Cyclopaedia* (1728). Meets d'Alembert. June: publishes *Philosophical Thoughts* (*Pensées philosophiques*) anonym-
ously; it is banned in July. Birth of François-Jacques-Denis.
Ordination of Didier-Pierre Diderot.

1747 June: denounced by the curé of Saint-Médard as 'a most
dangerous man', he is watched by the police. 16 October:
becomes joint director, with D'Alembert, of the *Encyclopaedia*
(*Encyclopédie*).

1748 Publication of his first novel, *The Indiscreet Jewels* (*Les Bijoux
indiscrets*). His sister Angélique dies in her convent. October:
death of his mother.

1749 24 July–3 November: imprisoned at the Château de Vincennes
for publishing the *Letter on the Blind* (*Lettre sur les aveugles*).
There he is visited by Rousseau. On his release, he meets
d'Holbach and Grimm.

1750 June: death of François-Jacques-Denis. October: birth of
Denis-Laurent, who dies in December. Distribution of the
Prospectus of the *Encyclopaedia*.

1751 18 February: *Letter on the Deaf and Dumb* (*Lettre sur les sourds
et muets*). 1 July: publication of volume i of the *Encyclopaedia*.

1752 January: volume ii of the *Encyclopaedia* which, together with
volume i, is banned by the Royal Council. The Prades affair
brings Diderot into conflict with the authorities. Police raid
his house. He entrusts other manuscripts to Malesherbes,
the government minister in charge of the book trade, for
safekeeping.

1753 November: volume iii of the *Encyclopaedia*. 2 September: birth
of Marie-Angélique, his fourth and only surviving child.
December: *Thoughts on the Interpretation of Nature* (*Pensées
sur l'interprétation de la nature*). Not wishing to provoke the
authorities, he publishes no more radical works until 1778.

1754 Volume iv of the *Encyclopaedia*. Begins following a course of
chemistry lectures.

1755 Volume v of the *Encyclopaedia*. Moves to the rue Taranne,
where he lives until shortly before his death. First of many

contributions appear in Grimm's *Literary Correspondence* (*Correspondance littéraire*). July: meets Sophie Volland (1716–84), who may have been his mistress for a time, and with whom he corresponded regularly for many years.

1756 May: volume vi of the *Encyclopaedia*. 29 June: Diderot's letter to Landois on determinism.

1757 February: publication of the play *The Natural Son* (*Le Fils naturel*) and the *Conversations about 'The Natural Son'* (*Entretiens sur le Fils naturel*), a discussion of the play and of Diderot's views on drama. March: beginning of the quarrel with Rousseau. November: volume vii of the *Encyclopaedia*.

1758 D'Alembert states his intention of withdrawing from the *Encyclopaedia*. October: Diderot breaks with Rousseau. November: the play *The Father of the Family* (*Le Père de famille*) and the *Discourse on Dramatic Poetry* (*Discours sur la poésie dramatique*).

1759 March: the permission to print the *Encyclopaedia* is withdrawn. 3 June: death of his father. September: the *Encyclopaedia* is condemned by Rome. Writes the first of his nine *Salons* (detailed accounts of the major art exhibitions in Paris, the last completed in 1781) for the *Literary Correspondence*.

1760 February–May: correspondence with the Marquis de Croismare, which becomes the starting point for *The Nun* (*La Religieuse*). 2 May: first performance of Palissot's satirical play *Les Philosophes*, which attacks him and the other leading philosophes.

1761 February: *The Father of the Family* is performed in Paris. Writes the *Eulogy of Richardson* (*Éloge de Richardson*), published in 1762. April (?): meets Jean-François Rameau, nephew of the composer. September: revises the last volumes of the *Encyclopaedia*.

1762 6 August: the Parlement orders the expulsion of the Jesuits. Works on *Rameau's Nephew* (*Le Neveu de Rameau*). D'Holbach introduces him to Laurence Sterne, who promises to send him the first six volumes of *Tristram Shandy*. The first of the eleven volumes of plates which accompany the *Encyclopaedia* appears: the last is published in 1772.

1763 Quarrels with his brother who, since 1745, had considered him the Antichrist. Meets David Hume.

1764 October: meets David Garrick. November: is furious to learn that his publisher Le Breton has secretly censored articles of the *Encyclopaedia*.

1765 Reconciled with D'Alembert, but Rousseau rejects his overtures. 1 May: Louis XV grants him permission to sell his library to Catherine II of Russia for 15,000 livres and an annual pension of 1,000 livres. She allows him to use it during his lifetime: it will revert to her only on his death. Autumn: reads volume viii of *Tristram Shandy* which contains the story of Trim's knee. Resumes, or more probably begins writing *Jacques the Fatalist* (*Jacques le fataliste*).

1766 Subscribers receive the remaining volumes (viii–xvii) of the *Encyclopaedia*.

1767 Diderot's brother appointed canon of the cathedral at Langres.

1769 August–September: writes *D'Alembert's Dream* (*Le Rêve de D'Alembert*). Falls in love with Mme de Maux.

1770 Writes a number of tales and dialogues, including *The Two Friends from Bourbonne* (*Les Deux Amis de Bourbonne*).

1771 Writes the *Philosophical Principles Concerning Matter and Movement* (*Principes philosophiques sur la matière et le mouvement*) and reads a version of *Jacques the Fatalist* to a friend. 26 September: *The Natural Son* staged in Paris. Diderot withdraws it after one performance.

1772 March: *On Women* (*Sur les femmes*). September: finishes two stories, *This is Not a Story* (*Ceci n'est pas un conte*) and *Madame de la Carlière*. Marriage of Angélique to an ironmaster, Caroillon de Vandeul.

1773 11 June: leaves Paris for Russia. 15 June–20 August: stays at The Hague, where he revises *Rameau's Nephew*, *Jacques the Fatalist*, and an article which would be published as *The Paradox of the Actor* (*Le Paradoxe sur le comédien*). Writes the *First Satire*. 8 October: arrives at St Petersburg.

1774 In Russia, he works on various writings dealing with politics, physiology, and materialism. 5 March: leaves St Petersburg, reaching The Hague on 5 April, where he remains until 15 September. Arrives in Paris on 21 October.

1776 A dialogue on atheism, the *Conversation of a Philosopher with the Maréchale de **** (*Entretien d'un philosophe avec la Maréchale de ****), appears in Métra's *Secret Correspondence* (*Correspondance secrète*).

1777 Continues his collaboration (1772–80) with the abbé Raynal in the *History of the Two Indies* (*Histoire des deux Indes*), writes a comedy, *Is he Good, is he Wicked?* (*Est il bon, est il méchant?*), and further revises *Rameau's Nephew* and *Jacques the Fatalist*.

1778 October: publication of the *First Satire* in the *Literary Correspondence*. November–June 1780: publication in serial form of *Jacques the Fatalist* in the *Literary Correspondence*.

1780 Revises *The Nun*, also serialized in the *Literary Correspondence*, and expands his *Essay on the Reigns of Claudius and Nero* (*Essai sur les règnes de Claude et de Néron*, 1778), his major political work.

1781 July: reads *Jacques the Fatalist* to his wife and probably makes further additions to the text.

1783 29 October: death of D'Alembert.

1784 22 February: death of Sophie Volland. The news is kept from Diderot, who is recovering from an attack of apoplexy. 15 July: moves to the rue de Richelieu. 31 July: death of Diderot. He is buried (1 August) in the church of Saint-Roch. 9 September: Catherine II sends 1,000 roubles to Mme Diderot.

1785 Friedrich Schiller translates the Mme de la Pommeraye episode of *Jacques the Fatalist* in *Die Rheinische Thalia*. This text is translated back into French by J.-P. Doray de Langrais in 1792 as *Strange Case of a Woman's Vengeance* (*Exemple singulier de la vengeance d'une femme*). 5 November: Diderot's library and manuscripts arrive in St Petersburg.

1792 *Jacques the Fatalist* translated into German by Christlob Mylius.

1796 Publication of *The Nun* and *Jacques the Fatalist*.

1805 Goethe publishes his translation of *Rameau's Nephew*.

Jean Baptiste Rameau,
Né a Dijon le 25 Septembre
1684.

Jean–Philippe Rameau walking in the gardens of the Palais-Royal.
C. L. Carmontelle, etching

(Jean-Philippe sometimes signed as Jean-Baptiste;
the year of birth given is incorrect.)

RAMEAU'S NEPHEW

Second Satire

*Vertumnis quotquot sunt natus iniquis**
(HORACE, *Satires*, II. vii)

RAMEAU'S NEPHEW

RAIN or shine, it's my habit, about five of an evening, to go for a stroll in the Palais-Royal.* It's me you see there, invariably alone, sitting on the d'Argenson bench, musing. I converse with myself about politics, love, taste, or philosophy. I give my mind licence to wander wherever it fancies. I leave it completely free to pursue the first wise or foolish idea that it encounters, just as, on the Allée de Foy, you see our young rakes pursuing a flighty, smiling, sharp-eyed, snub-nosed little tart, abandoning this one to follow that one, trying them all but not settling on any. In my case, my thoughts are my little flirts. If the weather's too cold, or too wet, I take refuge in the Café de la Régence,* where I pass the time watching the games of chess. Of all the cities in the world, it's Paris, and of all the places in Paris, it's the Café de la Régence, where chess is played best. Rey's café is the arena where the astute Legal, the subtle Philidor, the dependable Mayot mount their attacks; it's there that you witness the most astonishing moves and that you hear the most stupid conversation; for if one may be both a wit and a fine chess player like Legal, one may also be a fine chess player and an idiot like Foubert and Mayot. While I was there one evening, watching everything, not saying much and listening as little as possible, I was accosted by one of the most bizarre characters in this country, to which God has granted its fair share. He is a composite of nobility and baseness, good sense and irrationality. The concepts of honour and dishonour must surely be strangely jumbled in his head, for he makes no parade of the good qualities which nature has given him, and, for the bad, evinces no shame. He is, what's more, endowed with a strong constitution, an exceptionally vivid imagination, and an uncommonly powerful pair of lungs. If ever you meet him, and aren't stopped in your tracks by his singularity, then either you'll stick your fingers in your ears or you'll take to your heels. God, what terrible lungs. Nothing could be more unlike him than he

3

himself is. Sometimes he's thin and gaunt, like a consumptive on
his deathbed; you could count his teeth through the skin of his
cheeks. You'd think that he'd gone several days without food, or
just come out of a Trappist monastery. The following month he's
fat and paunchy, as if he'd never left the table of a tax farmer, or
had been confined in a Bernardine monastery. One day, in grubby
linen, torn breeches, and rags, virtually barefoot, he goes about
with his head down, avoiding people, and you'd be tempted to
call him over and slip him a coin or two. The next, powdered,
shod, curled, well dressed, he goes about with head high, he
wants to be noticed, and you'd be likely to take him for a gentleman, or near enough. He lives from day to day. Downcast or
cheerful, depending on the circumstances. His first concern, on
rising in the morning, is to determine where he'll have lunch;
after lunch, he considers where he'll go to dine. Night brings its
own anxieties. Either he'll return, on foot, to his tiny garret,
unless his landlady, weary of asking for his rent, has demanded
his key back; or he'll take refuge in an outlying tavern to await the
dawn over a crust of bread and a jug of beer. When he hasn't a
penny in his pocket, which happens from time to time, he resorts
to a friend who drives a cab or to a great lord's coachman, who
lets him sleep on the straw, beside the horses. The next morning
part of his mattress is still in his hair. If the weather's mild he
spends the night striding up and down the Cours-la-Reine or the
Champs-Elysées.* Dawn finds him back in the city, dressed in
yesterday's clothes for today, and occasionally for the rest of the
week. I hold such eccentrics in low esteem. Others seek out their
companionship, even their friendship. As for me, maybe once a
year I like to stop and spend time with them, because their character contrasts sharply with other men's, and they break with that
tedious uniformity which our education, our social conventions,
and our customary proprieties have produced. If one of them
appears in a group, he's like a grain of yeast that ferments, and
restores to each of us his natural individuality. He shocks us, he
stirs us up; he forces us to praise or blame; he brings out the
truth; he identifies honourable men and unmasks scoundrels; it

4

is then that the man of good sense keeps his ears open, and takes the measure of his companions.

I knew this one from a long while back. He frequented a household where his talents had made him welcome. An only daughter lived there. He used to swear to the mother and father that he'd marry the daughter. They'd shrug, laugh in his face, tell him he was crazy, yet I saw it actually happen. He'd ask me for a few écus, and I'd let him have them. He'd insinuated himself, by what means I do not know, into a number of respectable houses where he was given a seat at the dinner table, on condition that he never spoke without first asking permission. He would keep silent, and swallow his fury with his food. It was wonderful to see him thus constrained. Should he be tempted to break the treaty and open his mouth, at the first word all the guests would exclaim 'Oh! Rameau!' and his eyes would flash with rage as he set about swallowing his food even more furiously. You were curious to learn the name of the man; well, now you know it. He's the nephew of that famous musician who rescued us from Lully's plainchant, which we'd been droning out for over a hundred years; who wrote such reams of incomprehensible visions and apocalyptic verities on the theory of music, of which neither he nor anyone else ever understood a word, and who left us with a number of operas where we can enjoy various harmonies, unfinished songs, unrelated ideas, uproars, flights, triumphal fanfares, spears, ennoblements, seditious whisperings, endless victories; he also left us dance tunes that will live forever; he buried the Florentine, and will in his turn be buried by the Italian *virtuosi*; this he foresaw and it made him gloomy, depressed, cantankerous; for no one is as ill humoured, not even a pretty woman who wakes up with a pimple on her nose, as an author in danger of outliving his reputation—witness Marivaux and Crébillon the younger.

He addresses me: 'Aha! So it's you, Master Philosopher; and what are you doing here in this company of idlers? Wasting your time too, pushing the wood about?' (That's how the scornful refer to playing chess, or draughts.)

ME: No, but when I've nothing better to do, I enjoy spending a few minutes watching those who push it well.

HIM: In that case, you rarely enjoy yourself; apart from Legal and Philidor, the rest haven't a clue about the game.

ME: But what about Monsieur de Bissy?

HIM: That man's to chess, what Mademoiselle Clairon is to acting. Both have mastered everything that can be *learnt* about their respective playing.

ME: You're hard to please; I can see you'll allow nothing short of sublime perfection.

HIM: Yes, in chess, draughts, poetry, eloquence, music, and other such twaddle. What use is mediocrity in those genres?

ME: Very little, I grant you. But you need a great many people working in them to enable the man of genius to emerge. He's one in a million. But enough of that. It's ages since I saw you. I almost never think of you, unless I see you. But I'm always pleased when I do. What have you been up to?

HIM: What you, I, and everyone else are up to: good and bad, and nothing at all. Also I've felt hungry, and I've eaten, when I've had the chance; after eating, I've felt thirsty, and sometimes I've had a drink. Meanwhile, my beard's grown; and when it's grown, I've had it shaved.

ME: That was a mistake. It's the only thing you lack to make you a sage.

HIM: Yes, indeed. My forehead's high and furrowed; my eye full of passion; my nose hooked; my cheeks broad; my eyebrows black and bushy; my mouth well defined, with full lips; my chin square. If that enormous chin were covered with a long beard it would look very fine in bronze or marble, you know.

ME: Alongside a Caesar, a Marcus Aurelius, a Socrates.

HIM: No, I'd feel more at home between Diogenes and Phryne. I'm as shameless as the one and I'm a regular customer of the other.

ME: And you're still keeping well?

HIM: Yes, generally speaking, although not so wonderful today.

6

ME: Really? You've a paunch on you like Silenus's; and your face . . .

HIM: A face as fat as its posterior counterpart. That's because the ill humour that's shrivelling up my dear uncle seems to be fattening his dear nephew.

ME: Speaking of the uncle, do you ever see him?

HIM: Yes, in the street, in passing.

ME: Doesn't he help you out at all?

HIM: If ever he helps anyone, it's without being aware of it. In his own way he's a philosopher; he doesn't give a damn for the rest of the universe. His wife and daughter can go ahead and die whenever they like; as long as the parish bells, which will toll for them, continue to sound the twelfth and seventeenth intervals, all will be well. He's fortunate in that way; and it's what I value above all else in men of genius. They're good for one thing only. Other than that, nothing. They don't know what it means to be citizen, father, mother, brother, relative, friend. Just between you and me, one should imitate them in every way; but not wish the breed to be commonplace. We need men, but geniuses, no. No, my goodness, we don't need them. It is they who change the face of the world; and, even in the most trifling things, stupidity is so universal and so powerful that it can't be reformed without a great to-do. Part of their reform is carried out. The rest stays as before; result: two gospels, a two-coloured Harlequin costume. The wisdom of Rabelais's monk is the true wisdom, for his own peace and that of others: do your duty, after a fashion; always speak well of the Prior; and let the world live as it pleases.* This works well, since the majority is content with it. If I knew history, I'd show you that evil has always come into our world through some man of genius. But I don't know history, because I don't know anything. Devil take me if I've ever learnt a thing—and if, because I've never learnt a thing, I'm any the worse off. I was dining one day as the guest of one of the King's ministers, who's as clever as they come; well, he proved to us, as clearly as two and two make four, that nothing is more useful to the

7

common people than lies; nothing more harmful than the truth. I can't quite remember his proofs; still, the upshot is obviously that men of genius are detestable, and that if, at birth, a child bore on its forehead the stamp of this dangerous gift of nature, it ought to be smothered, or flung into the river with the rubbish.

ME: Yet those very people, who so hate genius, all consider themselves geniuses.

HIM: I'm certain that deep down that's how they see themselves, but they wouldn't dare admit as much.

ME: That's out of modesty. So you've conceived a fierce loathing of genius?

HIM: Which I'll never get over.

ME: But I remember a time when you despaired at being only an ordinary man. You'll never be happy if you find both alternatives equally distressing. You ought to decide what you want, then stick to it. While I agree with you that geniuses are usually odd, or, as the saying goes, 'you can't have a great mind without a little madness', you can't get away from the fact that centuries that have no geniuses are despised. Men of genius bring glory upon the nations that produced them; sooner or later statues of them will be erected, and they will be seen as benefactors of the human race. With all due respect to the sublime minister you cite, I believe that while a lie may have its uses at the present moment, in the long run it will cause harm, whereas, on the other hand, the truth will necessarily do good in the long run, although it may chance to cause harm at the present moment. From which I'd be tempted to conclude that the man of genius who discredits a commonly held error, or who upholds a great truth, is a man worthy of our veneration. Such a person might possibly be victimized by prejudice, or by the law; but there are two kinds of laws, laws whose equity and universality is absolute, and other, capricious laws, that owe their authority purely to blindness or to the constraints of circumstance. The latter bring only a passing ignominy upon the man who contravenes them, an ignominy which time then

8

transfers onto the judges and the nations involved, where it remains forever. Which of the two, Socrates or the magistrate who made him drink hemlock, is today the one dishonoured?

HIM: And a lot of good that did him! He was still convicted, wasn't he? Still put to death, still declared an agitator, wasn't he? In showing he despised a bad law, he still encouraged crackpots to despise good laws, didn't he? He was still a brazen, bizarre individual, wasn't he? You were almost at the point, just now, of admitting to an unfavourable opinion of genius.

ME: Listen, my friend. A society ought not to have bad laws, and if it had only good ones, it would never find itself persecuting a man of genius. I never told you that genius was inextricably linked to evil, nor evil to genius. A fool would be more likely to be bad than would an intelligent man. Even supposing that a genius were habitually hard to get on with, difficult, prickly, exasperating; even if he were truly evil, what would you conclude from that?

HIM: That he should be drowned.

ME: Calm down, my friend. Now, tell me this: I won't pick your uncle as an example; he's a hard man, a brute, devoid of human feeling; a miser. He's a bad father, a bad husband, a bad uncle; but it isn't certain yet that he's a genius, that he's taken his art a long way, and that his work will still be talked about ten years from now. But what about Racine? Unquestionably, *he* was a genius, yet he was not generally held to be all that good a man. What about Voltaire?

HIM: Don't rush me; I like to be consistent.

ME: Which would you prefer? That he'd been a good man, always busy with his bookshop, like Briasson, or with his bolts of cloth, like Barbier, giving his wife a legitimate child every year, a good husband; a good father, a good uncle, a good neighbour, an honest tradesman, but nothing more; or that he'd been a swindler, a traitor, ambitious, jealous, and spiteful, but had written *Andromaque*, *Britannicus*, *Iphigénie*, *Phèdre*, and *Athalie*?

HIM: My goodness, of the two, for him it might have been better to be the first.

9

ME: That's infinitely truer than you know.

HIM: Oh, you philosophers, there you go again! If something we say is to the point, it's by a fluke, because we're maniacs, or mystics. You and your friends are the only ones who know what you're saying. Yes, Master Philosopher, I know what I'm saying, and I know exactly the way you know.

ME: Well, let's see. Tell me: why for him?

HIM: Because all those fine things he wrote didn't put twenty thousand francs in his pocket, whereas if he'd been a good silk merchant in the Rue St Denis or the Rue St Honoré, a good wholesale grocer or a popular apothecary, he'd have made an immense fortune, and while making it there'd not have been any kind of pleasure that he wouldn't have enjoyed; because from time to time he'd have handed a gold coin to a poor devil of a buffoon like me who might have made him laugh, or occasionally procured him a young girl to relieve the monotony of the marriage bed; because we'd have enjoyed excellent meals at his table, and some serious gaming; drunk excellent wines, excellent liqueurs, excellent coffee; gone on pleasure jaunts outside the city—so you see, I knew what I was saying. You're laughing. But let me finish. It would have been better for those around him.

ME: Unquestionably: as long as he hadn't made a shameful use of the great wealth he'd acquired through honest trading: as long as he'd kept his house free of all those gamblers, those hangers-on, those mawkish yes-men, those idlers, those useless perverts, and had employed the underlings from his shop to beat up the officious character who provides husbands with a little relief from the unappealing monotony of the marriage bed.

HIM: Beat up! Beat up, Monsieur! No one is beaten up in a properly policed city. It's a respectable calling. Lots of people, even titled people, dabble in it. And what the devil do you want people to spend their money on, if not in keeping a good table, good company, good wines, beautiful women, and enjoying pleasures of every colour, diversions of every sort. I'd as soon be a beggar as possess a great fortune without any of those pleasures. But let's get back to Racine. That man was good only for men who were as yet unknown, and for centuries when he no longer existed.

ME: Agreed. But weigh the good and the bad. A thousand years from now he will stir men to tears, men in every country of the world will marvel at him. He will inspire benevolence, compassion, tenderness; men will ask who he was, where he came from, and will envy France because of him. He caused pain to some individuals who no longer exist, in whom we feel almost no interest; we ourselves have nothing to fear from either his vices or his failings. No doubt it would have been better had nature given him the virtues of a good man, together with the talents of a great man. He was like a tree in whose vicinity young trees shrivelled and died; he stifled the saplings growing at his feet; but his leafy crown touched the clouds and his branches stretched far and wide; he offered his shade to those who came, who come now and who will come to seek rest beside his majestic trunk; he produced fruit of an exquisite flavour that will never be exhausted. One might well wish that Voltaire had the sweetness of Duclos, the simplicity of Abbé Trublet, the rectitude of Abbé d'Olivet; but since that cannot be, let's look at the matter from the really interesting angle, let's forget for a moment the point we occupy in space and time, and extend our gaze to centuries that lie ahead, to lands far distant and to nations yet unborn. Let's reflect on the good of our own species. If we ourselves are insufficiently generous, let's at least forgive nature for having been wiser than we are. If you fling cold water on Greuze's head, you may perhaps wipe out his talent along with his vanity. If you make Voltaire less sensitive to criticism, he'll no longer be able to plunge into the depths of Mérope's soul.* He'll no longer move you.

HIM: But if nature is equally powerful and wise, why didn't she make them as good as they are great?

ME: But don't you see that such reasoning would turn the general order of things upside-down, and that if everything in our world were excellent, then nothing would be excellent?

HIM: You're right. The important point is that you and I should exist, and that we should be you and me. Let everything else get on as best it can. The best order of things, as I see it, is the one that includes me; to hell with the most perfect of worlds, if I'm not part of it. I prefer to be, and even to be an impudent logic-chopper, than not to be.

ME: But there isn't anyone who doesn't think like you, and who doesn't denounce the way the world works, without realizing that they're jettisoning their own existence.

HIM: That's true.

ME: So let's accept the way things are. Let's see what this costs us and what it gives us, let's not worry about the whole picture, which we don't know enough about to praise or censure, and which may well be neither good nor bad if, as many good people suppose, it's simply necessary.

HIM: Most of what you're talking about is beyond me. It sounds like philosophy; I warn you, I don't dabble in that. What I do know is that I'd love to be someone else, even at the risk of being a man of genius, a great man. Yes, I have to admit, there's something that makes me feel that way. I've never heard anyone praised without secretly feeling wild with envy. I'm an envious man. When I hear some discreditable detail about their private life, I'm delighted. It brings us closer. I find my mediocrity easier to bear. I tell myself: Of course you'd never have written *Mahomet*,* but neither would you have written that eulogy to Maupeou.* So I have been, and I still am, discontented with being mediocre. Yes, oh yes, I'm mediocre and discontented. I've never heard the overture to *Les Indes galantes* being played, never heard 'Profonds abîmes du Tenare', 'Nuit, éternelle nuit'* being sung, without telling myself gloomily: you'll never write such music. So I was jealous of my uncle, and if at his death there'd been some beautiful harpsichord music among his manuscripts, I wouldn't have hesitated to go on being me and be him as well.

ME: If that's all that's upsetting you, it's hardly worth it.

HIM: It's nothing. These moments quickly pass. [Then he

again started humming the overture to *Les Indes galantes* and the melody of 'Profonds abîmes' before continuing:] That whatever–it–is inside me that speaks to me says: Rameau, you'd love to have written those two pieces; if you'd written those pieces, you'd undoubtedly do two more, and when you'd done a certain number, they'd be playing and singing you every-where; you'd walk with your head high, and you'd hear your conscience testifying to your own worth; others would point you out. They'd say: 'He's the man who wrote those charming gavottes.' [Here he began humming the gavottes, then, with the air of a man deeply moved, as if overcome with joy, his eyes full of tears, he added, rubbing his hands:] you'd have a good home [and with his arms he measured out the size], a good bed [and he stretched nonchalantly out on it], good wines [which he savoured, clicking his tongue against his palate], a good carriage [and he raised his leg as if stepping up into it], pretty women [whose breasts he was already fondling as he eyed them lustfully]; a hundred hangers-on would come every day and flatter me [and he seemed to be watching them gather round him: Palissot, Poinsinet, the Frérons both father and son, and La Porte; he was listening to them arrogantly, nodding approval and smiling, then waving them away with a sneer, only to summon them back again; then he continued:] And so they'd tell you in the morning that you're a great man; you'd read in *Three Centuries of our Literary Heritage** that you're a great man; by evening you'd be convinced that you're a great man; and the great man, Rameau the nephew, would fall asleep to the sweet murmur of praises ringing in his ears; even asleep he'd look pleased with himself; his chest would dilate and rise and fall freely; he'd snore, like a great man [and saying this, he let himself subside indolently onto a bench; he closed his eyes, and imitated the happy sleep he was imagining. After enjoying this pleasurable repose for a few moments, he awoke, stretched his arms, yawned, rubbed his eyes, and looked around again for his insipid toadies].

ME: So you believe the happy man sleeps soundly.

HIM: Do I believe it! A poor devil like me, when I'm back in my attic at night and tucked into my cot, I lie shrivelled up under my blanket; my chest's constricted and my breathing's constrained; the ear can barely detect a kind of feeble groaning, whereas the breathing of a financier shakes the walls of his room and astounds his entire street. But what troubles me today is not that my snores and my sleep are so niggardly, like some wretched beggar's.

ME: But that is sad, even so.

HIM: What's happened to me is far sadder.

ME: So what is it, then?

HIM: You've always taken a certain amount of interest in me, because I'm quite a good sort of devil whom in your heart you despise but find amusing.

ME: Quite true.

HIM: So I'm going to tell you. [But first, he sighs deeply and rests his forehead on both his hands. Then, somewhat calmer, he says to me:] You know I'm a stupid, crazy, cheeky, lazy ignoramus, what we Burgundians call a bad lot, a swindler, a glutton . . .

ME: What a panegyric!

HIM: It's the exact truth. There's not a single inaccurate word. I'll thank you not to question any of it. Nobody knows me better than I do; and I'm not telling everything.

ME: I don't want to annoy you; I'll agree with every point.

HIM: Well, I was living with some people who'd taken a liking to me, precisely because I possessed—to an exceptional degree—all those qualities.

ME: This is extraordinary. Up till now I'd supposed that one concealed such defects from oneself, or forgave oneself for them while despising them in others.

HIM: Conceal them from oneself, is that possible? You can be sure that when Palissot's on his own, thinking about himself, he tells himself something different. You can be sure that when he's alone with his partner, they freely admit to one another that they're just a couple of out-and-out swindlers. Despise

14

them in others! My people were fairer than that, their character was such that I was a marvellous success with them. I was in clover. They spoiled me rotten. They missed me if I was gone for a single moment. I was their dear little Rameau, their pretty Rameau, their clownish, crazy, cheeky, ignorant, lazy, greedy, gross Rameau. There was not one of those familiar epithets that did not earn me a smile, a caress, a cuff on the shoulder, a slap, a kick, or, at table, a tasty morsel flung onto my plate. Away from the dinner table they behaved with a certain freedom that I thought of no consequence, for I'm a man of no consequence. They did what they pleased of me, with me, in front of me, without offending me; and then—those little presents they showered me with! How could I have been so unbelievably crass—I've lost it all! I've lost it all because once, just once in my life, I showed some ordinary good sense—ah, never ever again!

ME: But what happened?

HIM: An unparalleled example of the most inexcusable, irremediable folly.

ME: But what sort of folly?

HIM: Rameau, Rameau, that wasn't what they'd taken you in for! The folly of showing a little good taste, a little wit, a little judgement. Rameau, my friend, that'll teach you to stay the way God made you and your patrons wanted you. So they grabbed you by the shoulders, marched you to the door, and said: 'Get out, you rat, and don't ever come back. I do believe the creature's trying to show it's intelligent, it has a mind! Get out! Besides, those are things we already have.' So out you went, biting your fingers; it was your cursed tongue you should have bitten, earlier. Because you didn't grasp that, there you were, standing outside in the cold, not a penny in your pocket, not knowing where to turn. You were fed like a turkey-cock, and now you're back to the slop-house; you were well housed, and now you'll be lucky to get your attic back; you had a comfortable bed, and now you'll sleep on straw, between Monsieur de Soubise's coachman* and our friend

Robbé. Instead of a sweet, peaceful sleep, like you used to enjoy, in one ear you'll be hearing the whinnying and stamping of horses; in the other, the infinitely more insufferable sound of harsh, wooden, unpolished verses. You miserable, reckless, devil-driven wretch!

ME: But is there no way to get back into their favour? Was your offence so unpardonable? If I were you, I'd go there and see them. They need you more than you realize.

HIM: Oh! I'm sure that now they haven't got me there to make them laugh, they're bored to tears.

ME: So I'd go and see them. I wouldn't leave them time to get used to doing without me and find some respectable entertainment; for who can say what might not happen?

HIM: That's not what I'm afraid of. That'll never happen.

ME: However extraordinary your talents may be, someone else could replace you.

HIM: With difficulty.

ME: Agreed. Nevertheless, I'd go to see them with your face a wreck, your eyes staring, your collar bedraggled, and your hair a mess, in short with that positively tragic air you're displaying at this very moment. I'd cast myself at the feet of the goddess. I'd press my face into the ground; without getting up, I'd say in a low, heartbroken voice: 'Forgive me, madame, forgive me! I'm a worthless, vile wretch. It was but a fleeting mistake; for you know that I am not usually given to showing good sense, and I promise you that I never, ever, will do so again.'

The amusing thing was that, while I was telling him this, he was suiting his actions to my words. He'd flung himself down and was pressing his face into the ground; his hands seemed to be clutching at the tip of a slipper; he was weeping, and sobbing, and saying: 'Yes, my sweet queen, I promise you this; never again in my whole life, never again.' Then, suddenly standing up, he added in a serious, thoughtful tone:

HIM: Yes, you're right. I believe that's best. She's kind. Monsieur

Vieillard says that she's so kind. I've seen some of it myself. And yet, to have to toady to that dreadful bitch! Beg for mercy from a wretched second-rate player whom the pit loves to hiss off the stage! I, Rameau, son of Monsieur Rameau, the Dijon apothecary, a man of substance, who's never called anyone Master! I, Rameau, nephew to the man known as the great Rameau, whom one sees walking in the Palais-Royal, holding himself erect, his arms swinging freely, ever since Monsieur Carmontel sketched him bent double with his arms tucked under the skirts of his jacket!* I, who have composed pieces for the harpsichord which nobody plays, but which may be the only ones to survive and be played by posterity; I, Rameau in person! That I should go . . .! Look, Monsieur, it simply can't be. [And placing his right hand on his heart, he added:] I feel something rising up here and telling me: Rameau, you'll do nothing of the kind. It's essential that man's nature comprise a certain dignity, which nothing can stifle. A mere trifle can arouse it. Yes, a mere trifle. Then there are other times when I'd happily be as vile as you could wish; at such a time it wouldn't cost a penny to get me to kiss little Hus's arse.

ME: But look here, my friend: it's white, young, pretty, tender, plump; it's an act of humility that a more fastidious man than you might stoop to on occasion.

HIM: Let's get this clear: there's kissing arses literally, and kissing arses figuratively. Ask that fat Bergier, who kisses Madame de La Marck's arse both literally and figuratively; and, upon my word! in that particular case I'd find both equally unpleasant.

ME: If the plan I've suggested isn't to your liking, then have the courage to be a pauper.

HIM: It's hard to be a pauper, when there are so many wealthy halfwits one could live off. And then to despise oneself: that's unbearable.

ME: But have you ever experienced that emotion?

HIM: Of course I have; how many times have I said to myself: for God's sake, Rameau, there's ten thousand well-served tables in Paris, each with fifteen to twenty places set; of those places,

17

there isn't a single one for you! Purses are overflowing with gold on every side, and not one coin falls your way! A thousand little so-called wits without talent or merit, a thousand charmless little creatures, a thousand mean and petty schemers go about in finery, and you are naked? You're as big a fool as that? Can't you flatter as well as the next fellow? Don't you know how to lie, swear, perjure yourself, promise, break or keep your word, like the next fellow? Don't you know how to get down on all fours, like the next fellow? Don't you know how to ease the way for Madame's little affair, and deliver Monsieur's *billet doux*, like the next fellow? Don't you know how to encourage that young man to speak to Mademoiselle, and persuade Mademoiselle to listen to him, like the next fellow? Don't you know how to hint to the daughter of a bourgeois that she's badly turned out; that a pair of lovely earrings, a touch of rouge, some lace, and a dress *à la polonaise* would suit her to perfection? That those dainty feet of hers weren't made to walk on pavements? That there's a handsome gentleman, young and wealthy, with a gold-laced coat, a splendid carriage, and six tall footmen, who saw her as he passed by and found her enchanting; that since that day he cannot eat, or drink, or sleep, and so will surely die of love . . . 'But my papa!' 'Well, yes, your papa! He'll be rather cross at first . . .' 'And mama, who's forever exhorting me to be a good girl? Who tells me that the only thing that matters in this world is my honour? . . .' 'Oh, those are meaningless old-fashioned notions . . .' 'And what about my father confessor? . . .' 'You won't see him any more; or if you insist on telling him of your diversions, it'll cost you a few pounds of sugar and coffee . . .' 'He's very strict; he's already refused me absolution for singing that song: "Come into my cell" . . .'* 'That's because you had nothing to give him . . . but when he sees you wearing lace . . .' 'So I'll be wearing lace?' 'Certainly, lace of every variety; and beautiful diamond earrings . . .' 'So I'll have beautiful diamond earrings?' 'Yes . . .' 'Like those of that Marquise who sometimes buys gloves in our shop? . . .' 'Exactly . . . in an elegant carriage, drawn by a pair of dapple-greys; two tall footmen, a little black boy, a runner in front, rouge, patches, someone to carry your train . . .' 'At a ball? . . .' 'At a ball, at the opera, at the theatre . . .' Her heart is already leaping for joy. 'Your fingers are fiddling with a sheet of paper. What is it?' 'Oh, it's nothing.' 'But what is it?' 'It's a note.' 'Who's it for?' 'It's for you, if you were the slightest bit interested.' 'Interested . . . I'm very interested. Let me see . . .' She reads. 'A meeting, that's impossible.' 'Perhaps on your way to mass . . .' 'Mama always goes with me; but if he came here, quite early; I get up first, and I'm behind the counter before anyone's about . . .' He comes, he pleases; one fine day, at twilight, Mademoiselle vanishes, and I collect my two thousand écus . . . And here you are with a talent like that, and yet you can't find yourself a decent meal! Aren't you ashamed, you pathetic creature? I could recall a dozen rogues who didn't hold a candle to me, but had purses full to bursting. There I was in a coat of coarse linen, while they were wearing velvet; they leaned on gold-handled canes, their fingers loaded with splendid diamond rings. And yet what were they? For the most part miserable music hacks; now they're gentlemen, of a sort. So then I'd feel full of courage; my spirits soaring, my mind razor-sharp, capable of anything. But it seems that this positive attitude never lasted, for up until now I've made no headway. However that may be, you now know the subject of my habitual soliloquies: make of them what you will, as long as you conclude that I am indeed familiar with self-contempt, that torment of the conscience you suffer if you fail to use those talents Providence bestowed on you; it's the cruellest of all torments. One almost feels it would have been better not to have been born.

As I listened to him describing the scene of the procurer seducing the young girl, I found myself torn between two conflicting emotions, between a powerful desire to laugh and an overwhelming surge of indignation. I was in agony. Again and again a roar of laughter prevented my rage bursting forth; again and again the rage rising in my heart became a roar of laughter. I was dumb-founded by such shrewdness and such depravity; by such sound-ness of ideas alternating with such falseness; by so general a perversity of feeling, so total a corruption, and so exceptional a candour. He saw how agitated I was. 'What's the matter?' he asked.

ME: Nothing.

HIM: I think you're upset.

ME: Indeed I am.

HIM: So what do you think I should do?

ME: Talk about something else. What a wretched fate, to have been born or to have fallen so low!

HIM: I agree. But don't let my state affect you too much. In open-ing my heart to you, it was not my intention to upset you. I've managed to save a little, while I was with those people. Remem-ber I wanted for nothing, nothing whatsoever, and they also made me a small allowance for incidentals. [Here he began to strike himself on the forehead with his fist, bite his lips, and roll his eyes like a lunatic, then he said:] What's done is done. I've put a bit aside. Time's passed, so I'm that much to the good.

ME: You mean to the bad.

HIM: No, to the good. Live one day less, or have one écu more, it's all the same. The important thing is to open your bowels easily, freely, enjoyably, copiously, every evening; *o stercus pretiosum!** That's the grand outcome of life in every condition. At the final moment, we are all equally rich—Samuel Bernard who by dint of theft, pillage, and bankruptcy leaves twenty-seven million in gold, and Rameau who'll leave nothing, Rameau for whom charity will provide the winding-sheet to wrap him in. The corpse doesn't hear the bells tolling. It's in vain that a hundred priests bawl themselves hoarse for him, it's in vain that he's preceded and followed by a long line of mourners bearing flaming candles; his soul does not process beside the master of ceremonies. Rotting under marble or rotting under earth, you're still rotting. Whether you've choirboys in red and

blue surplices around your coffin or no one at all, what difference does it make? And then just look at this wrist: it was stiff
as the devil. These ten fingers were like rods stuck into a
wooden metacarpus; these tendons were like old catgut cords
that were drier, harder and more unyielding than those driving
a turner's wheel. But I tormented them, I worked them, I
broke them. You don't want to do it; well by God I'm telling
you you'll do it; and you shall.

While he was speaking he had grasped the fingers and wrist of his
left hand with his right and forced them up, then down, so that
the tips of the fingers were touching his arm; the joints began to
crack and I feared he might dislocate the bones.

ME: Careful; you'll damage yourself.
HIM: Don't worry. They're used to it; for the last ten years I've
given them a really bad time. In spite of themselves, the stub-
born devils have had to get used to it, and learn how to place
themselves on the keys and to dart about on the strings. So
now they work. Yes, they work.

Saying this, he assumes the posture of a violinist; he hums an
allegro of Locatelli's; his right arm mimics the movement of the
bow, while his left hand and fingers seem to travel up and down
the neck; if he plays a wrong note he stops, tightens or loosens the
peg, then plucks the string with his nail to check that it's in tune;
he takes up the air again where he left off, beating time with his
foot while his head, his feet, his hands, his arms, his entire body
continue their frenetic activity. Occasionally, at the Concert spirituel,* you've seen Ferrari or Chiabrano or some other *virtuoso* go
through the same gyrations; they create an image of this same
torture, and watching them, I feel this same pain; for is it not
painful to watch the agonies suffered by someone trying to portray pleasure? Let a curtain conceal this man from me, if he has to
show me a victim being put to the torture. If, in the midst of his
agitation and his cries, if he came to a slow, sustained phrase, one

of those melodious passages where the bow slowly moves over several strings at once, his face would assume an ecstatic expression, and his voice grow softer as he listened rapturously to himself, knowing with certainty that the harmonies were resounding in my ears as well as in his own. Then, with the hand that held his instrument, he tucked it back under his left arm, and let his right hand, the bow still in it, fall. 'Well, how was it?' he asked me.

ME: Superb.

HIM: It'll do, I think; it sounded pretty good, as good as other people.

And then he promptly squatted down, like a musician seating himself at the harpsichord. 'Please, don't—for both our sakes,' I said to him.

HIM: No, no; since I've got you, you're going to listen to me. I've no use for plaudits I haven't earned. You'll praise me more confidently, and that'll attract a pupil or two.

ME: I go about in society so rarely, you'll tire yourself for nothing.

HIM: I never get tired.

Realizing that it was pointless to feel sorry for the fellow—the violin sonata had left him drenched in sweat—I decided to let him go ahead. So there he was, seated at the harpsichord, legs bent, head up, gazing at the ceiling as if to read there the notes of a score, singing, trying this and that, and then playing a composition by Alberti, or Galuppi, I'm not sure which. His voice sang like the wind, his fingers flew over the keys, sometimes dropping the treble for the bass, sometimes abandoning the accompaniment and picking up the melody again. His features revealed the play of successive emotions: tenderness, fury, pleasure, pain. You could tell when he was playing *piano*, when *forte*. And I'm certain that a more accomplished man than I would have recognized the piece, by its tempo and character, by the expressions on his face and by a few snatches of song that occasionally escaped him. But the curious thing was that at times he'd stumble in his playing, then correct himself as if he'd played a wrong note, and felt upset at no longer having the piece at his fingertips. 'There, as you can see,' he said, standing up and wiping the drops of sweat that were trickling down his cheeks, 'we also know the correct use of augmented fourths and fifths, and are quite familiar with dominant progressions. Those enharmonic modulations my dear uncle made such a to-do about aren't really that difficult: we manage.'

ME: You've gone to a great deal of trouble to show me how highly skilled you are, but I was quite prepared to take your word for it.

HIM: Highly skilled? Oh no! As regards my profession, I know more or less what I'm doing, which is more than what's required. Is there any obligation, in this country, to know the subject one teaches?

ME: No more than to know the subject one studies!

HIM: By God that's right, that's exactly right. Now, Master Philosopher, place your hand on your heart and tell me honestly: wasn't there a time when you were not as well off as you are today?

ME: I'm still not all that well off.

HIM: But now, in summer, you wouldn't still go to the Luxembourg Gardens—you remember?

ME: Let's not talk about that; yes, I remember.

HIM: In a shaggy grey coat.

ME: Yes, yes.

HIM: Worn threadbare on one side, the cuffs torn, and your stockings of black wool with the seams darned in white.

ME: Yes, yes, whatever you say.

HIM: So, back then, what were you doing in the Allée des Soupirs?*

ME: Cutting a rather pathetic figure.

HIM: And once outside the Gardens, you'd be pounding the pavement.

ME: I agree.

HIM: You used to give mathematics lessons.

ME: Without knowing a thing about the subject, isn't that what you're getting at?

HIM: Exactly.

ME: I learnt by teaching others, and I turned out some good students.

HIM: That may be, but music isn't the same as algebra or geometry. Now you're a big fish.

ME: Not so very big.

HIM: And doing very nicely, thank you.

ME: Not all that nicely.

HIM: You're hiring masters to teach your daughter.

ME: Not yet. It's her mother who sees to her education: you have to have peace at home.

HIM: Peace at home? My goodness, you only have peace if you're either servant or master, and the one to be is master. I had a wife, God rest her soul, but if she occasionally got uppish with me I'd get on my high horse and thunder at her, I'd say, like God: 'Let there be light!' and there was light. And in all four years we didn't raise our voices at each other so many as ten times. How old is your child?

ME: That's got nothing to do with it.

HIM: How old's your child?

ME: Devil take it, let's leave my child and her age out of it, and get back to the tutors she'll be having.

HIM: God, I've never met anything as pigheaded as a philosopher. In all humility, I wish to enquire of My Lord Philosopher if one might possibly ascertain the age of Mademoiselle his daughter.

ME: Let's say she's eight.*

HIM: Eight! Then she ought to have had her fingers on the keyboard for the last four years.

ME: But perhaps I didn't particularly wish to include in her education a subject that takes up so much time and is of so little use.

HIM: So what are you planning to teach her, may I ask?

ME: If I can, to think straight—a very rare thing among men, and even more so among women.

HIM: Let her think as illogically as she wants, as long as she's pretty, amusing, and knows how to please.

ME: Since nature has been so unkind to her as to give her a delicate constitution along with a sensitive soul, and to expose her to the same pain in life as if her constitution were strong and her heart made of bronze, I'll teach her, if I can, to bear her pain courageously.

HIM: Let her weep, suffer, simper, and complain of her nerves like all the others, as long as she's pretty, amusing, and knows how to please. What, no dance lessons?

ME: No more than what's required to master curtseying, deportment, how to handle herself correctly, and how to walk well.

HIM: No voice lessons?

ME: No more than what's required to learn proper pronunciation.

HIM: No music lessons?

ME: If I could find a good tutor for harmony, I'd be happy to have him teach her a couple of hours a day, for a year or two, but no more than that.

HIM: And in the place of those essentials you're eliminating?

ME: I'll put grammar, mythology, history, geography, a little drawing, and a great deal of ethics.

HIM: How easily I could prove to you the uselessness of all those subjects in a world like ours; indeed, not simply the uselessness, but perhaps even the danger. But for the moment I'll content myself with this question: won't she need a tutor or two?

ME: Undoubtedly.

HIM: Now we're back on our subject. And these tutors, you expect them to know grammar, mythology, history, geography, ethics, which they'll teach her? Nonsense, my dear sir, nonsense. If they knew those subjects well enough to teach them, they wouldn't be doing so.

ME: Why not?

HIM: Because they'd have spent their entire life learning them. You have to have completely immersed yourself in art or in science to understand its fundamental principles. The classic

25

texts are only interpreted well by those who've grown old in their perusal. It's the middle and the end that illuminate the shadows of the beginning. Ask your friend Monsieur D'Alembert, the leading luminary of mathematical science, whether he would be too expert to teach its rudiments. It was only after thirty or forty years of study that my uncle began to see glimmers of light in the darkness of musical theory.

ME: Oh, you king of all fools [I exclaimed], how does it come about that that no-good head of yours contains such sound ideas all scrambled together with such wildly extravagant notions?

HIM: Who the devil knows? Chance puts them into your head, and there they remain. It therefore follows that unless you know everything, you really know nothing. You don't know where one thing's going; where another comes from; where this or that one should be put; which one should come first or would be better placed second. Can you teach something properly without a method? And a method, where does that originate? Listen, my philosopher friend, it strikes me that physics will always be a weakling science, a drop of water from the vast ocean caught up on the point of a needle, a grain of dust from off the Alps; and then, what about the causes of phenomena—truly, it would be better to know nothing than to know so little, so imperfectly; and that's exactly the point I'd reached when I became a teacher of accompaniment and composition. What are you thinking about?

ME: I'm thinking that everything you've just said is more specious than solid. But enough of that. You've taught, you say, accompaniment and composition?

HIM: Yes.

ME: And you knew nothing whatever about them?

HIM: Believe me, I knew nothing; and that's why there were some worse than me: those who believed they knew something. At least I didn't spoil either the taste or the hands of the children. When they went from me to a good teacher, as they had learnt nothing they at least had nothing to unlearn; which meant that much money and time saved.

ME: How did you manage?

HIM: The way they all do. I'd arrive. I'd fling myself into an armchair ... 'What dreadful weather! The streets are so exhausting!' I'd pass on a few bits of gossip. 'Mademoiselle Lemierre was to play a vestal virgin in that new opera, but she's pregnant for the second time. No one knows who's to be her understudy. Mademoiselle Arnould's just broken with her little count.* They say she's negotiating with Bertin. However, the little count has discovered the secret of Monsieur de Montami's porcelain. At their last concert the Friends of Music had an Italian woman who sang like an angel.* That Préville's a rare bird. You really must see him in *Le Mercure galant*,* the bit about the enigma's a riot. That poor Dumesnil hasn't a clue what she's saying or what she's doing. Come on, Mademoiselle, get your book.' While Mademoiselle, who's in no hurry, hunts for her book which she's mislaid, and a chambermaid's summoned, and Madame scolds, I continue: 'La Clairon is quite incomprehensible. There's talk of a totally preposterous marriage—it's that Mademoiselle—now whatever *is* her name—that little thing he was keeping, by whom he's had two or three children, and who'd been kept by all those others ...' 'Come now, Rameau, it's not possible, you're talking nonsense.' 'No, it's not nonsense. They say it's actually taken place. There's a rumour that Voltaire's dead. What good news.' 'Why good news?' 'Because that means he's about to let loose some splendid sally. It's his custom to die a couple of weeks beforehand. Let's see, what else was there?' I'd tell a few smutty anecdotes I'd heard at the houses where I'd just been, for we're all of us great scandalmongers. I'd play the fool. They'd listen to me, they'd laugh. They'd exclaim: 'Still such a charmer!' Meanwhile Mademoiselle's book would have turned up under an armchair where it had been dragged, chewed and torn by a puppy or perhaps a kitten. She'd sit down at her harpsichord. She'd begin to make a noise all by herself. Then I'd draw nearer, after nodding my approval to the mother. The mother: 'It's not going badly; she just needs to exert herself a little, but exertion's the last thing on her mind. She'd rather waste time chattering, messing with her clothes, rushing about, doing goodness knows what. The door's barely shut behind you but the book's closed, and isn't reopened until you come again. And you never tell her off . . .' As some action was called for, I'd take her hands and reposition them on the keyboard. I'd get cross and shout: 'G, G, G, Mademoiselle, it's G!' The mother: 'Mademoiselle, have you no ear? Even I, who am not at the instrument, and can't see your book, I feel it's a G that's wanted. You're giving Monsieur Rameau so much trouble. His patience is beyond belief. You don't remember a thing he tells you. You're making no progress at all . . .' I'd then temper the blows somewhat and, with a nod, would say: 'Excuse me, Madame, excuse me, things could be better, if Mademoiselle made an effort, if she studied a little, but it's not going badly.' The mother: 'If I were you I'd keep her on the same piece for an entire year . . .' 'As to that, she won't master it until she's overcome all the difficulties; but that won't take as long as Madame supposes . . .' The mother: 'Monsieur Rameau, you're flattering her; you're too kind. That's the only thing she'll remember from her lesson, and she'll be sure to repeat it to me when the need arises . . .' The hour would pass. My student would hand me my fee, with the graceful gesture and curtsey her dancing master taught her. I'd put it into my pocket, while the mother said: 'Very nice, Mademoiselle; if Javillier were here, he'd applaud you.' I'd chat a little longer out of politeness, then I'd slip away; that's what used to be called a lesson in accompaniment.

ME: And is it any different today?

HIM: Lord, I think so. I arrive. I look serious. I quickly deposit my muff. I open the harpsichord. I run my fingers over the keys. I'm always in a hurry. If I'm kept waiting for a minute, I protest loudly, as though I were being robbed: 'An hour from now I have to be at such and such a house; two hours from now the Duchess of X expects me. I'm engaged for dinner with a beautiful marquise, and when I leave there, I'm going to a concert at Baron de Bagge's house, in the Rue neuve des Petits-Champs.'

ME: But you're not really expected anywhere?

HIM: True.

ME: So why go in for those base little subterfuges?

HIM: Base? Why base, may I ask? They're standard in my calling. I'm not degrading myself by doing as everyone else does. It wasn't I who invented them, and I'd be strange and maladroit not to use them. Of course I know quite well that if you apply to what I've described certain general principles of God knows what morality that people talk about all the time but never put into practice, what is white will be black, and what is black will be white. But, Master Philosopher, there exists such a thing as a universal conscience. Just as there's a universal grammar; and then there are exceptions in every language that you experts call, I believe, well . . . give me a hint, will you? . . . you call them . . .

ME: Idioms.

HIM: Exactly. Well now, every calling has its exceptions to the universal conscience, which I'd like to call the idioms of that calling.

ME: I understand. Fontenelle speaks well and writes well, although his style teems with French idioms.

HE: And the sovereign, the minister, the financier, the magistrate, the soldier, the man of letters, the lawyer, the public prosecutor, the merchant, the banker, the craftsman, the singing master, the dancing master, are perfectly respectable people, although their conduct deviates in several respects from the universal conscience, and abounds in moral idioms. The more ancient an institution, the greater the number of its idioms; the worse the suffering in a particular age, the more the idioms multiply. The man is worth what his occupation is worth, and vice versa; in the final analysis, their worth is the same. So people make their own occupation seem as significant as possible.

ME: What I'm hearing clearly through that tangle of words is that there are few honourably exercised occupations, or that there are few honourable men exercising them.

HIM: Alright, we'll agree there are none at all; but on the other hand, there are few who are scoundrels outside of their shop; and everything would go on quite nicely were it not for certain individuals who are called hardworking, reliable, punctilious in their duties, strict, or what amounts to it; always in their shop, working at their job from dawn to dusk, and doing nothing else. Result: they're the only ones to earn a fortune, and a fine reputation.

ME: Through force of idiom.

HIM: Exactly. I see you're with me. Now, an idiom common to all conditions—for there are idioms common to all nations and all ages, just as there are common follies—a common idiom is to acquire as large a clientele as possible; a common folly is to believe that the most capable man is the one with the most clients. There you have two exceptions to the rule of universal morality which we must accept. It's a kind of good will. It doesn't mean much in itself, but it acquires value through public opinion. There was a saying that 'a fine reputation was worth more than a belt of gold'. However, a man with a fine reputation may not own a gold belt, whereas nowadays I see that someone who owns a gold belt seldom lacks a fine reputation. One should, as far as possible, possess both the reputation and the belt. And that is my object when I resort to what you call cheap tricks, base little subterfuges. I teach my lesson, and I teach it well; that's the absolute standard. I make people believe that I still have more lessons to get to than there are hours in the day. That's the idiom.

ME: And you really do teach well?

HIM: Yes, not badly, tolerably well. The ground-bass theory of the dear uncle has made everything much simpler. In the past I used to steal my pupil's money: yes, I stole it, no doubt about that. Today I earn it, at least as well as others do.

ME: And did you steal it without any qualms?

HIM: Oh, without any qualms. You know the saying: 'if one thief steals from another, the devil laughs.' The parents were dripping with money acquired God knows how; they were courtiers, tax farmers, wholesalers, bankers, businessmen. I helped them to make restitution, I and countless others who, like me, were employed by them. In nature all the species prey on one another; in society all the classes do the same. We mete out justice to one another without benefit of the law. La Deschamps in the past, and today la Guimard, avenge the King by cheating the tax farmer; it's the dressmaker, the jeweller, the upholsterer, the linen maid, the swindler, the lady's maid, the cook, the harness-maker, who avenge the tax farmer by cheating la Deschamps. Amidst all this, only the imbecile or the idler suffers a loss without exacting his price from someone else: which only serves him right. Whence you may deduce that these exceptions to the universal conscience, or these moral idioms people make such a fuss about, labelling them illicit benefits, are of no consequence; the only thing that matters is to see clearly.

ME: I admire that in you.

HIM: And then there's poverty. The voice of conscience and of honour sounds very faint when the belly screams. I'll simply say that if ever I grow rich, I will certainly have to make restitution, and I'm quite determined to do so by all possible means—by feasting, by gaming, by drinking, by women.

ME: But I'm afraid you'll never grow rich.

HIM: That is what I too suspect.

ME: But if it were to happen, what then?

HIM: I'd behave like every beggar on horseback: I'd be the most insolent rogue ever seen. I'd then remember everything they'd made me suffer, and I'd pay them back in spades for their affronts. I love bossing people about and I'll boss them about. I love praise, and they'll praise me. I'll have the whole gang of Villemorien's minions in my pay, and I'll order them, just as I've been ordered: 'Come on, you rats, amuse me', and they'll amuse me; 'give me the dirt on all the decent people', and they'll do so, if any such are still to be found; and we'll go whoring; we'll call one another *tu* when we're drunk, and we shall get drunk; we'll pass on scurrilous gossip; we'll indulge in

31

all kinds of profligacy and vice. It'll be absolutely delicious. We'll prove that Voltaire has no genius, that Buffon, who's always on his high horse, is just a pompous ranter; that Montesquieu is nothing but a wit;* we'll tell D'Alembert to stick to his sums and we'll give a really good going-over to all those petty stoics like you, who despise us out of envy, cloak their pride in modesty, and live soberly out of necessity. And music? Ah, then indeed we'll have music!

ME: Considering the worthy use you'd make of wealth, it seems to me deplorable that you should be penniless. Such a lifestyle would reflect great honour on the human race, be of great service to your fellow citizens, and reflect great glory upon you.

HIM: I rather think that you're making fun of me; but, Master Philosopher, you don't understand whom you're dealing with; you've no idea that at this moment I represent the most significant section of the Town and the Court. The very wealthy in every social group either have or have not told themselves these very same things that I've confided to you; but the fact remains that the life I'd lead were I in their shoes is precisely the life they do lead. Just take a look at what you believe. You people imagine that everyone seeks the same kind of happiness. What a strange fantasy! Your happiness presupposes a certain romantic mindset that the rest of us don't share, an exceptional kind of spirit, particular tastes. You adorn this oddity with the label of virtue, you call it philosophy. But are virtue and philosophy suited to everybody? Enjoy them if you can. Be true to them if you can. Imagine the world wise and philosophical; you must agree that it would be devilishly dreary. Listen—let's give a cheer for philosophy, and one for wisdom: the wisdom of Solomon. Drinking fine wines, eating one's fill of choice dishes, tumbling pretty girls, sleeping on soft beds—except for these, all else is vanity.*

ME: What! Defending your country?

HIM: Vanity. It's no longer *your* country. From pole to pole I see only tyrants and slaves.

ME: Helping your friends?

HIM: Vanity. Have you any friends? And supposing you had, should you risk making ingrates of them? Consider carefully: you'll realize that almost always ingratitude is what you get for helping them. Gratitude is a burden, and all burdens are made to be cast off.

ME: Holding a position in society and fulfilling its responsibilities?

HIM: Vanity. What does it matter whether you have a position or not, as long as you're rich, since you only take a position in order to become so? Fulfilling your responsibilities, what does that get you? Jealousy, problems, persecution. Is that the way to get on in the world? Pay court, for God's sake, pay court; frequent the powerful, study their tastes, fall in with their whims, serve their vices, applaud their wrongdoing. That's the secret.

ME: Seeing to your children's education?

HIM: Vanity. That's the responsibility of a tutor.

ME: But supposing that tutor were a follower of your principles and neglected his duties, who would pay the penalty?

HIM: Not I, that's certain; some day, possibly, my daughter's husband, or my son's wife.

ME: But if they were both to sink into a life of debauchery and vice?

HIM: That's in keeping with their position.

ME: And if they were disgraced?

HIM: If you're rich, no matter what you do, you can't be disgraced.

ME: And supposing they were ruined?

HIM: That's their bad luck.

ME: It seems to me that if you don't take responsibility for the conduct of your wife, your children, or your servants, you might easily neglect your own affairs.

HIM: Excuse me, but you're mistaken; it's sometimes difficult to lay one's hands on money, and so it's prudent to look ahead.

ME: But you wouldn't bother much about your wife.

HIM: Not at all, in fact. The best possible policy, I believe, in dealing with one's better half is to do what pleases her. In your

33

opinion, wouldn't society be extremely entertaining if we all did our own thing?

ME: Why not? I never think my evening so delightful as when I've enjoyed my morning.

HIM: That's true of me too.

ME: What makes society people so finicky about their diversions is their complete idleness.

HIM: Don't you believe it. They're constantly on the go.

ME: Because they never get tired, they can never feel refreshed.

HIM: Don't you believe it. They're always worn out.

ME: They pursue pleasure because it keeps them busy, never because they feel the need of it.

HIM: So much the better; need is always an affliction.

ME: They use everything up. Their soul becomes stupefied. Boredom takes possession of it. He who would deprive them of life at the height of their burdensome plenty would be doing them a favour. They know only that part of happiness which loses its edge most rapidly. I don't despise the pleasures of the senses. I too have a palate, which delights in a delicate dish or a delectable wine. I have a heart and I have eyes: I love looking at a pretty woman. I love to feel beneath my hand the firmness and roundness of her breast, to press my lips to hers, to drink in the sensuality of her gaze, and to die of ecstasy in her arms. Occasionally, when I'm with friends, an evening of wine and women, even if it's somewhat wild, does not displease me. But I won't conceal from you that I find it infinitely sweeter to have helped the unfortunate, concluded a thorny negotiation, given useful advice, read an agreeable book, taken a walk with a man or a woman dear to my heart, spent some instructive hours with my children, written a satisfying page, fulfilled the duties of my station, or to have told my beloved of sweet and tender feelings which induced her to wrap her arms round my neck.* There are certain things I would give everything I own to have done. *Mahomet* is a sublime work; but I would rather have rehabilitated the memory of Calas.* An acquaintance of mine had taken refuge in Carthagenia. He was a younger son, in a

34

country where custom dictates that all property pass to the eldest. While abroad he hears that his elder brother, a spoilt youth, has robbed his too-credulous father and mother of everything they possess, cast them out of their chateau, and left the good old people quite destitute, to languish in some small provincial town. So what does that younger son do? Harshly treated by his parents in the past, he had departed to seek his fortune in a distant land: he sends them money, and quickly settles his own affairs. He returns a very wealthy man. He restores his parents to their home. He arranges marriages for his sisters. Ah, my dear Rameau, this man thinks of that period of time as the happiest in his life. It was with tears in his eyes that he told me of it; and my heart, as I tell you this story, overflows with joy, and happiness renders me speechless.

HIM: How odd you are, you people!

ME: And how greatly you people are to be pitied, if you can't believe that one can rise above good or ill fortune, and that it's impossible to be unhappy, when one is protected by fine deeds like these.

HIM: That's a kind of happiness with which I'd find it hard to become familiar, for it is very rare. So, the way you see it, one must be an honourable man?

ME: To be happy? Unquestionably.

HIM: Nevertheless, I know countless honourable people who aren't happy, and countless people who are happy without being honourable.

ME: That's what you think.

HIM: And isn't it because, for just a moment, I showed some common sense and honesty that I don't know where to find my dinner this evening?

ME: Oh no, it's because you haven't always shown them. It's because you didn't understand straight away that first and foremost one must secure a livelihood that is independent of servitude.

HIM: Independent or not, the livelihood I secured is surely the least demanding.

35

ME: And the least dependable, and the least honourable.

HIM: But the most consonant with my character of idler, fool and good-for-nothing.

ME: Agreed.

HIM: And furthermore, since I can secure my happiness by means of vices which come naturally to me, that I've acquired without labour and preserved without effort, which suit the ways of my country, conform to the tastes of my protectors, and are more appropriate to their special little needs than virtues which would embarrass them by making them feel ashamed all day long; it would be extremely odd were I to torment myself like a soul in hell, to become something other than what I am, and develop a character quite alien to my own; highly estimable qualities, I admit, to avoid argument, but which I'd find exceedingly difficult to acquire and to practice, which would get me nowhere, perhaps worse than nowhere, by continually showing up the rich from whom beggars like myself seek to earn their livelihood. The world praises virtue, but loathes it and flees from it; virtue is left out in the cold, and in this world one must keep one's feet warm. And then, it would be certain to put me out of humour; for why do devout people so often strike us as so hard, so difficult, so unsociable? It's because they've set themselves a task which doesn't come naturally. They suffer, and when you suffer, you make others suffer. That doesn't suit me, nor does it suit my patrons; I have to be light-hearted, adaptable, entertaining, clownish, amusing. Virtue demands respect, and respect is uncomfortable. Virtue demands admiration, and admiration isn't funny. I spend my time with people who get bored, and it's my job to make them laugh. Now, absurdity and folly are what make people laugh, so I must be absurd, and a fool; if nature had not given me those qualities, then the simplest solution would be to pretend to possess them. Luckily I have no need to be a hypocrite, since there are already so many of every hue, apart from those who are hypocrites with themselves. That chevalier de la Morlière who wears his hat with upturned brim tipped over one ear, sticks his nose in the air and stares over his shoulder at every passer-by, who carries a long sword that thumps against his thigh, has an insult ready for anyone not thus armed, and seems to challenge every man he meets, what's he doing? He's doing his utmost to persuade himself that he's brave, but he's really a coward. Tweak the end of his nose and he'll take it meekly. If you'd like him to lower his tone, raise yours. Show him your cane, or let your foot connect with his buttocks: astonished at discovering he's a coward, he'll ask you who it was that told you, or where you found it out. He himself was unaware of it a moment earlier; his ingrained habit of aping the brave had deceived him. He had so often adopted the posture that he believed he was the real thing. And that woman who mortifies herself, visits prisons, attends every charitable assembly, walks with lowered gaze, not daring to look a man in the face lest she let down her guard against the seduction of the senses; does all that prevent her heart from burning, does it prevent her sighs escaping, or her passions quickening, her desires tormenting her, or her imagination from replaying, by day as by night, scenes from *Le Portier des Chartreux*, or the positions described in Aretino?* So then what happens to her? What does her maid think as she jumps out of her bed in her shift, and flies to help her mistress who cries out that she's dying? Justine, go back to bed. It's not you your mistress is calling for in her delirium. And, were our friend Rameau some day to disdain fortune, women, fine dishes, idleness, and turn stoic, what would he be? A hypocrite. Rameau must be what he is: a lucky rogue among wealthy rogues, and not a trumpeter of virtue, or even a virtuous man, gnawing his crust of bread alone or in a company of beggars. And, in a word, I am not settling for your felicity, nor for the happiness of a few visionaries like yourself.

ME: I see, my friend, you don't know what I've been talking about, and you're not even capable of learning about it.

HIM: All the better, the Lord be thanked, all the better. It would make me croak from hunger, boredom, and perhaps from remorse.

37

ME: So, in view of that, the only advice I have for you is to get back quickly inside the house from which you so imprudently got yourself thrown out.

HIM: And to do what you don't disapprove of in a literal sense, but I find rather repugnant in a metaphorical sense.

ME: That's my advice.

HIM: Independently of that metaphor which offends me at this moment, and at some other moment won't.

ME: How odd you are!

HIM: There's nothing odd about it. I'm quite willing to be abject, but I want to be abject without constraint. I'm quite willing to lower my dignity . . . you're laughing.

ME: Yes, your dignity makes me laugh.

HIM: Everyone has his dignity; I'm quite willing to forget mine, but when *I* choose, and not at someone else's bidding. Why should anyone be able to say: 'Grovel!' and I be forced to grovel? Grovelling's natural to the worm, and to me; that's what we both do when we're left to our own devices; but we rear up when we're stepped on. I've been stepped on, and I intend to rear up. And then you've no idea what a bear garden the place is. Picture to yourself a gloomy, sullen individual, perpetually prey to the vapours, enveloped in two or three layers of dressing gown; he takes no pleasure in himself, he takes no pleasure in anything else; to raise the merest hint of a smile one must deploy physical and mental gyrations of a hundred different varieties; he observes the funny contortions of my features and those of my intellect—which are even funnier—with equal impassivity; just between ourselves, that père Noël, that ugly Benedictine who's so famous for his grimaces, well, in spite of his success at court, and in all due modesty and fairness, compared with me he's nothing but a wooden puppet. It's in vain that I try to emulate the exquisite grimaces of lunatics; nothing works. Will he or won't he laugh? That's what I have to ask myself in the midst of my contortions, and you can imagine how badly this uncertainty affects my performance. My hypochondriac, his head buried in a nightcap coming down to his eyes, looks like a motionless Chinese idol from beneath whose chin a string hangs, leading down under his chair. One waits for the string to be pulled, but it is not pulled; or, if the jaw happens to open slightly, it's to utter some disheartening words, words which tell you that you have not been noticed, and that all your antics are wasted; the words answer a question you asked several days ago; once they are uttered, the mastoid spring relaxes and the jaws snap shut . . .* [Then he began to mimic his man; he settled into a chair, head rigid, hat pulled down to his eyelids, eyes half closed, arms hanging loosely, jaw moving, mouthing, like an automaton: 'Yes, you're right, Mademoiselle. Subtlety, that's what is needed.'] That's what decides, that's what always decides, irrevocably, in the morning, in the evening, while dressing, at dinner, at the café, at the gaming tables, at the theatre, at supper, in bed, and, God forgive me, I do believe in the arms of his mistress. I'm not in a position to hear these last decisions, but I'm damnably tired of the others. Gloomy, inscrutable, and final as fate: that's our *patron*.

Opposite him, there's a prude who puts on important airs and to whom one forces oneself to say that she's pretty, because she is, still, although there's a few scabs on her face, and she's vying with Madame Bouvillon in the fat stakes. I'm fond of a bit of flesh, when it's nicely rounded, but enough is enough, and movement is vital to matter! *And*: she's nastier, prouder, and stupider than a goose. *And*: she tries to be witty. *And*: you have to make her believe you think her wittier than anyone else. *And*: she knows nothing, but that doesn't stop her laying down the law. *And*: you must applaud these pronouncements with your feet, with your hands, leap for joy, faint with amazement. How beautiful, delicate, well expressed, discerning, how extraordinarily sensitive! Whence comes this ability that women possess? It's unstudied, it's sheer force of instinct, it's a powerful natural gift: it's almost a miracle! Just let someone dare assert that experience, study, reflection, education, play any part in it! And other nonsense of that sort: then come tears of joy. Ten times a day you must bow, one knee bent forward, the other leg stretched back, your arms extended towards the goddess, your eyes fixed on hers to discover her wishes; you must hang on her words, await her bidding, then depart in a flash. Who can subject himself to the demands of such a role, except the wretch who finds in that house, two or three times a week, what he needs to calm the torment in his belly? What is one to think of the others, like Palissot, Fréron, the Poinsinets, Baculard, who aren't destitute, and whose grovelling can't be excused by the rumbling of their tortured guts?

ME: I'd never have supposed you to be so fastidious.

HIM: I'm not fastidious. At first I watched the others, and I did what they did, or even improved on it a little, because I'm more openly impudent, a better actor, more ravenous, blessed with better lungs. Evidently I'm a direct descendant of the famous Stentor.

And, to give me a clear idea of the power of that organ, he began coughing so violently that it rattled the panes of the café windows, and distracted the chess players from their game.

ME: But what's the use of that talent?

HIM: You can't guess?

ME: No. I haven't much imagination.

HIM: Imagine that an argument is in full swing and my victory is uncertain: I rise, and, deploying my thunder, say: 'It's just as Mademoiselle has declared. That's what I call judgement! I defy any of our best minds to equal it. The expression is pure genius.' But you mustn't always give your approval in the same manner. You'd become boring. You'd sound false. You'd lack piquancy. You can only avoid that by judgement and inventiveness; you have to know how to prepare and situate these imperious major keys, how to grasp the opportunity and the moment; for instance, when opinions are divided, and the argument has reached boiling-point, people are no longer listening but are all speaking at once; then you must distance yourself, take up your position in the corner of the room farthest from the battlefield, prepare for your thunderbolt by a long silence, and suddenly launch it like an exploding mortar into the thick of the battle. No one can equal me in this art. But where I am astonishing is in the opposite situation: I can draw on a range of soft tones that accompany a smile; on an infinite variety of approving expressions, working now the nose, now the mouth, now the forehead, now the eyes; I've a particular pliancy of the hips; a way of contorting the spine, of raising or dropping the shoulders, of spreading the fingers, of nodding the head and closing the eyes, of registering amazement, as if I'd heard a divine, angelic voice issuing from heaven. That's the way to flatter. I'm not sure you fully grasp how much energy goes into this last charade. It's not my invention, but no one has surpassed me in its performance. See? See?

ME: It's true, it's quite unique.

HIM: Do you believe any female mind inclined to vanity could resist that?

ME: I have to agree that you've carried the talent of playing the lunatic, and of degrading yourself, to its farthest possible extreme.

HIM: Whatever they try, every last one of them, they'll never equal that. The best of them, Palissot for example, will never be more than a good student. But although the game's amusing at first, and one takes a certain pleasure in privately deriding those whom one befuddles, in the long run it loses its savour; and then, also, after coming up with a few new ideas, one is obliged to repeat oneself. Wit and art have their limits. There's only God or a handful of rare geniuses for whom the way ahead stretches endlessly on, as they move forward along it. Bouret may be one of those. There are certain traits of his which give me—yes, me—a sense of the sublime. The little dog, the Register of Felicity, the flaming torches on the road to Versailles, they're the kind of things which confound and mortify me. They're enough to discourage one from trying.

41

ME: What are you talking about, what little dog?

HIM: Where have you been all this time? Do you really not know how this extraordinary man set about detaching from himself and attaching to the Minister of Justice the affections of a little dog that had caught the minister's fancy?

ME: I do not know, I confess.

HIM: Good. It's one of the most beautiful stories anyone could imagine; all of Europe marvelled at it, and there isn't a single courtier whose envy it did not excite. You're a shrewd man; let's see how you'd have gone about it. Remember that Bouret's dog loved him. Remember that the minister's bizarre costume frightened the little animal. Remember that Bouret only had a week to solve the difficulties. You must be aware of all aspects of the problem to fully appreciate the merit of the solution. Well?

ME: Well, I must admit to you that in this kind of situation I'd be incapable of solving the simplest difficulty.

HIM: Listen [he tapped me lightly on the shoulder as he spoke, for he likes taking little liberties], listen, and marvel. He gets himself a mask made in the likeness of the Minister of Justice; he borrows the voluminous cassock from a valet. He covers his face with the mask. He puts on the cassock. He calls his dog, pats him, gives him a biscuit. Then suddenly, after changing his accoutrements, it's no longer the Minister of Justice, it's now Bouret that calls his dog and beats him. In less than two or three days of continually performing this drill from dawn to dusk, the dog has learnt to flee from Bouret the tax farmer, and run to Bouret the Minister of Justice. But I'm being too kind. You're a non-believer who doesn't deserve to be instructed in the miracles which take place right under your nose.

ME: Nevertheless, I entreat you—the book, the flaming torches?

HIM: No, no. Enquire of the pavingstones, they'll give you those details; you should be making the most of our chance meeting to hear of things no one knows but me.

ME: You're right.

HIM: Borrow the gown *and* the wig; I forgot the wig, the wig of the Minister of Justice! To get a mask made in his likeness! The mask, above all else, makes my head spin. Of course the man enjoys the highest reputation. Of course he's a millionaire. There are military officers with the Cross of St Louis who want for bread, so why exert oneself to get a Cross, at the risk of life and limb, rather than choose a safe calling which never fails to be rewarded. That's what's called aiming at true greatness. Such examples are discouraging; they make you feel sorry for yourself, and bored with life. The mask! The mask! I'd give one of my fingers to have thought of the mask.

ME: But, with your passion for the finer things of life, and your inventive mind, have you yourself created nothing new?

HIM: Excuse me, indeed I have. For instance, that admiring inclination of the spine I mentioned; I consider it mine, although the envious might dispute my claim. I agree that it's been used before, but did anyone appreciate how it enabled you to enjoy a laugh at the expense of the fool you were admiring? I know a hundred ways to set about seducing a young girl, with her mother at her side, without the latter being aware of it; I can even turn her into an accomplice. Hardly had I begun my career than I disdained all the routine devices for passing on *billets doux*. I know ten ways to make the girl snatch it away from me, and among those ways I dare to flatter myself that some are entirely new. I'm particularly good at encouraging a timid young man; I've seen some succeed who lacked both looks and wit. If this were written down, I think I'd be recognized as something of a genius.

ME: People would hold you in great esteem.

HIM: I don't doubt it.

ME: Were I in your place, I'd scribble these things down on paper. It would be a pity if they were lost.

HIM: True; but you've no idea how little importance I attach to method and precepts. He who must follow instructions will never get far. Geniuses read little, do a lot, and create themselves. Look at Caesar, Turenne, Vauban, the Marquise

43

de Tencin, her brother the cardinal, and the cardinal's secretary, Abbé Trublet. And Bouret? Who taught Bouret? No
one. It's nature that teaches those exceptional men. Do you
imagine the story of the dog and the mask is written down
somewhere?

ME: But when you've nothing to do, when the pangs of your
empty stomach or the travails of your overburdened stomach
keep you from sleeping . . .

HIM: I'll think about it; it's better to write of great deeds than
to perform trivial ones. They uplift your soul, they stir,
inspire, and expand your imagination, whereas your imagination shrivels when you have to pretend, when you're with
little Hus, that you're astonished by the applause a half-witted
public obstinately showers on that simpering Dangeville; her
style of acting is insipid, she walks about the stage bent right
over, she's so affected, the way she gazes all the time into her
interlocutor's eyes while standing right under his nose, and
imagining that the faces she's pulling are subtle acting, and
that her mincing gait's really graceful; and as for that bom-
bastic Clairon! She's skinnier, stiffer, stagier, starchier than I
can find words for. That idiotic parterre applauds them to the
skies, without noticing the bundle of charms that *we* are—a
bundle that's getting a bit fatter, it's true—but who cares?
They don't notice that our skin's quite exquisite, our eyes
absolutely beautiful, our mouth very pretty; admittedly we've
no real heart, and we're a bit heavy-footed, but not as awkward
as some would claim. When it comes to emotions, on the other
hand, there's no one who comes a close second.

ME: What do you mean, exactly? Are you being ironic, or sincere?

HIM: The trouble is that these devilish feelings are all inside,
there's not a gleam showing outside. But you can take my word
for it, I know, I know very well that they're there. If not precisely emotions, then something of that sort. You should just
see, when we're in a bad mood, how we treat the valets, how the
maids get slapped, how we administer our boot to the Private
Parts of the Treasury if it deviates in the slightest from the

respect due to our person. She's a little devil, I tell you, full of feeling and dignity . . . so, now, you haven't any idea what I'm talking about, have you?

ME: I confess that I can't tell whether what you're saying is sincere or spiteful. I'm a simple soul: I wish you'd say what you mean to me and not bother about being clever.

HIM: Well, that's what I dish out to little Hus about la Dangeville and la Clairon, with the odd word slipped in to put you wise. I can take your thinking me a good-for-nothing, but not a fool, and only a fool or a man besotted with love would seriously profess so much nonsense.

ME: But how can you bring yourself to utter this nonsense?

HIM: It doesn't happen all at once, you get there one step at a time. *Ingenii largitor venter.**

ME: Surely one would have to be driven by dreadful pangs of hunger.

HIM: Possibly. However, no matter how egregious you may think it, you must understand that those to whom the nonsense is addressed are more accustomed to hearing it than we are to saying it.

ME: Is there anyone living there brave enough to think as you do?

HIM: What do you mean by anyone? That's how the whole of society feels and speaks.

ME: Those of your circle who are not utterly worthless must be complete and utter fools.

HIM: Fools? In that house? I swear to you there's only one: the man who is host to all of us in exchange for our deceiving him.

ME: But how can he let himself be so grossly deceived? After all, no one disputes the genuinely superior gifts of la Dangeville and la Clairon.

HIM: One drinks up a flattering lie in great gulps, whereas a bitter truth one sips drop by drop; and then, we appear to be so utterly convinced, so sincere.

ME: But surely, you must at some time have sinned against the principles of your art and let slip one or two of these bitter, hurtful truths; for in spite of the wretched, abject, vile, abominable role you fill, I believe that deep down you have a sensitive soul.

HIM. Me? Not in the least. Devil take me if I have the faintest idea of what I really am. In general, my mind's as uncomplicated as a sphere and my character as candid as a flower; never false if it's in my interest to be true, and never true if it's in my interest to be false. I say whatever comes into my head, if it's sensible, so much the better, but if it's pointless, no one pays attention. I make good use of my freedom of speech. Never once in my life have I thought before speaking, while speaking, or after speaking. So I never offend anyone.

ME: Still, you actually did so in the case of those good people you were living with, who'd treated you so well.

HIM: What do you expect? It was unfortunate, an unlucky moment, life's full of them. Happiness can't last; I was doing too well, it couldn't go on. As you know, the company there is numerous and most select. It's a school of benevolence, a return to the hospitality of ancient times. Every fallen playwright is welcomed with open arms. We had Palissot after his *Zara*,* Bret after *Le Faux généreux*,* as well as every unsuccessful musician, every unread author, every actress that's hissed and every actor that's booed; a bunch of shameful wretches, insipid parasites at whose head I have the honour to stand, the valiant leader of a timorous band. It is I who exhorts them to eat the first time they come; it's I who makes sure that their glass is filled. They take up so little room, a few shabby young men who don't know which way to turn, but look presentable enough, and some others, real rogues, who play up to their host and earn his trust, so that they can go gleaning in his wake in the fields of their hostess. We seem a cheerful lot, but in reality we're all angry, and fiercely hungry. Wolves are not more ravenous, nor tigers more cruel. We devour the way wolves do, when the ground has long been under snow; we tear asunder, as tigers do, anything that meets with success. Occasionally, the Bertin, Monsauge, and Vilmorien gangs join forces: then indeed the din in the menagerie is worth hearing! Never have there been gathered together so many surly, cantankerous, malevolent, and enraged animals. All one hears are the names of Buffon, Duclos, Montesquieu, Rousseau, Voltaire, D'Alembert, Diderot, accompanied by God only knows what kind of epithets. No one credited with the least intelligence, unless he's as stupid as we are. That's how the idea for *Les Philosophes** came into being; I'm responsible for the scene about the book peddler, after the style of that play about the lady theologian.* You weren't spared in it any more than anyone else.

ME: Good. Perhaps they do me greater honour than I deserve. I'd be mortified if those who disparage so many clever, decent men were to speak well of me.

HIM: There are lots of us, and we must each do our bit. Once we've sacrificed the larger beasts, we make offerings of the others.

ME: To live by insulting learning and virtue—that's a high price to pay for your daily bread!

HIM: I've already told you, we're of no importance. We insult everyone and hurt no one. Sometimes we have that ponderous Abbé d'Olivet and the fat one, Le Blanc, also that hypocrite Batteux. The fat Abbé is only spiteful before dinner. After he's drunk his coffee, he flings himself into an armchair, props up his feet against the chimney-piece, and falls asleep like an old parrot on its perch. If the din gets very loud, he'll yawn, stretch his arms, rub his eyes, and say: 'What's going on? What's going on?' 'We're trying to decide whether Piron's wittier than Voltaire.' 'Let's be clear. It's wit you're talking about? Not taste? Because if it's taste, your Piron hasn't any idea what that is . . .' 'No idea?' 'No . . .' And we're off on a disquisition about taste. Then our host signals to us to listen—for he believes himself an authority on taste. 'Taste,' he says, 'taste is something . . .' God, I don't know what he said it was, and neither does he.

Sometimes our friend Robbé turns up. He treats us to his cynical stories about the convulsionaries and their miracles,

47

which he's actually witnessed with his own eyes, as well as to recitations of a few cantos of his poem on a subject he knows thoroughly. I detest his poetry but I love hearing him recite. He seems almost possessed. All around him you hear cries of: 'Now that's what I call a poet!' Just between you and me, that kind of poetry is nothing but a charivari of cacophonies, the uncouth cackle of inhabitants of the Tower of Babel.

We are also visited by a certain simple-looking fellow who gives the impression of being dull and stupid, but who possesses a savage wit, and is craftier than an old monkey: one of those faces that invite jokes and jeers, and were designed by God for the castigation of men who judge by appearances. Their mirror should have taught them that it's as easy to be clever and look a fool as it is to be a fool behind a clever face. It's such a common act of cowardice to hand over a good man to the ridicule of others that people never fail to have a go at this one. It's a trap we set up for new arrivals, and I've hardly seen a single one escape being caught.

Sometimes the accuracy of my madman's observations on men and their natures surprised me; I told him so. 'It's because,' he replied, 'you can learn from bad company, just as you can from debauchery. You're compensated for your loss of innocence by the loss of your prejudices. In bad company, where vice wears no disguise, you learn to recognize such people; and then, I've read a bit.'

ME: What have you read?
HIM: I've read, am reading, and constantly reread Theophrastus, La Bruyère, and Molière.
ME: Excellent writers.
HIM: They're a lot better than is generally believed; but who knows how to read them?
ME: Everyone, to the best of his ability.
HIM: Almost no one. Could you tell me what people seek in them?

48

ME: Entertainment and instruction.

HIM: But what sort of instruction, that's the point!

ME: To recognize one's duties, to love virtue, to hate vice.

HIM: For my part, I find in them a digest of everything one *ought* to do, and everything one *ought not* to say. Thus, when I read *L'Avare*, I tell myself: be miserly, if you wish, but take care not to talk like the miser. When I read *Tartuffe*,* I tell myself: be a hypocrite, if you wish, but don't talk like a hypocrite. Keep those vices which serve you well, but beware of the tone and the air that go with them, and would make you appear ridiculous. To be sure of avoiding that tone and air, one must know what they are; now, those authors have portrayed them superbly. I am myself, and that is what I shall remain; but I behave and talk in a socially acceptable manner. I'm not one of those men who despise the moralists. One can profit greatly from them, particularly from those who depict morals in action. Vice itself is only intermittently shocking. The appearance of vice is shocking at all times. Perhaps it would be better to be an arrogant fellow than to look like one; the man with the arrogant character offends only from time to time; the man with the arrogant face offends all the time. And by the way, you shouldn't suppose that I'm the only reader of this kind. The sole merit I claim here is having accomplished systematically, through clear thinking and rational, accurate observation, what the majority of others do by instinct. That's why their reading doesn't make them better than me, but instead, they go on being ridiculous, whereas I am so only when I mean to be, and then I leave them far behind me; for the same art that shows me how to avoid ridicule in certain situations, shows me also, in other situations, how to achieve it at a superior level. Then I bring to mind everything others have said, everything I've read, and I add everything of my own invention, which in this domain is surprisingly abundant.

ME: You were wise to reveal these mysteries to me, as otherwise I would have thought you contradictory.

HIM: No, that's not so; because for every occasion when one must avoid inviting ridicule, there are fortunately a hundred others where ridicule is called for. In high society there's no better role to play than that of fool. For centuries the king had his officially appointed fool, but never an officially appointed sage. I'm Bertin's fool and the fool of many others, perhaps yours at this moment—or you, perhaps, are mine. A true sage wouldn't have a fool. So it follows that he who has a fool is not a sage; if he's not a sage, he's a fool; and perhaps, if he were king, the fool of his fool. Anyway, remember that in a subject as variable as manners and morals, nothing is absolutely, essentially, universally true or false, unless it is that one must be whatever self-interest dictates, good or bad, wise or foolish, seemly or ridiculous, honest or vicious. If by chance virtue had been the path to wealth, either I'd have been virtuous or pretended to be so, like everyone else. I was required to be ridiculous, so I made myself ridiculous; as to vicious—nature took care of that entirely by herself. When I say vicious, I'm using your vocabulary; for, were we to talk this through, it might turn out that what you call vice I call virtue, and virtue what I call vice.

At the house we also meet authors who write for the Opéra-Comique,* and their actors and actresses; and, even more frequently, their managers Corby, Moette—all of them men of wealth and outstanding merit.

And I was forgetting the great literary critics, *L'Avant-Coureur*, *Les Petites Affiches*, *L'Année littéraire*, *L'Observateur littéraire*, *Le Censeur hebdomadaire*,* the whole gang of hired hacks . . .

ME: *L'Année littéraire*, *L'Observateur littéraire*—impossible! They loathe one another.

HIM: But it's true. All the down-and-outs make it up at the feeding trough. That damned *Observateur littéraire*. To hell with him, and all his sheets of newsprint! It's that undersized cur of a miserly, malodorous, moneylending priest who's the cause of my disaster. Yesterday he made his first appearance on the scene. He arrived at the hour that brings us all out of our lairs, the dinner hour. When the weather's bad, if one of us can come up with a coin for a cab, he's lucky. Occasionally someone makes fun of a fellow guest who arrives thick with mud from head to foot and soaking wet, only to find himself in a similar state when he returns home. There was one a few months back, I don't recall his name, who got into a violent row with the boot-black who'd been hanging about our entrance. They'd had some business deals together; the creditor wanted his debtor to pay up, but the latter was not in funds, and couldn't. Dinner is served; the Abbé's treated as the guest of honour and seated at the head of the table. I enter, I notice him. 'So, Abbé,' I say to him, 'you're presiding? That's fine for today, but tomorrow you'll please move down one place, and the next day another place; and in this way, place by place, either on the left side or the right, until, from the place that I occupied—once— before you, and Fréron once after me, Dorat once after Fréron, Palissot once after Dorat, you'll become a fixture next to me, a poor dull fool like you, *qui siedo, sempre comme un maestoso cazzo fra due coglioni*.'* The Abbé, who's a good-humoured soul and takes everything in good part, began to laugh. Mademoiselle, struck by the truth of my observation and the aptness of my comparison, began to laugh; all those seated to the Abbé's right and left, and whom he had shifted down a notch, began to laugh; everyone laughed, except Monsieur, who was annoyed, and spoke to me in a way that wouldn't have mattered had we been alone: 'Rameau, you're impertinent . . .' 'I know I am; that's the requirement for my being here . . .' 'A cad . . .' 'No worse than the next man . . .' 'A down-and-out . . .' 'Why else would I be here . . .' 'I'll have you thrown out . . .' 'I'll leave of my own accord, after dinner . . .' 'I think you'd be wise . . .' We had dinner; I didn't miss a single bite. After dining well and drinking copiously—for after all it was neither here nor there, and there's never been bad feeling between Messer Gaster* and myself—I made up my mind and prepared to leave. I'd given my word in the presence of such a large gathering that I had no choice but to keep it. I spent quite a time wandering round the room, hunting for my cane and hat in the wrong places, all the while expecting the *patron* to launch into a fresh torrent of invective, someone to intervene, and that we'd make it up in the end, having exhausted our anger. I wandered back and forth, for I had no cross feelings to work off, but the *patron*'s looks were gloomier and blacker than those of Homer's Apollo when he loosed his arrows against the Greek warriors; he was striding up and down the room with his cap pulled down even further than usual and his fist supporting his chin. Mademoiselle came up to me. 'Mademoiselle, what's so extraordinary about what I did today, how have I been any different from usual?' 'I want him to go.' 'I *am* going, but I haven't really offended him.' 'Excuse me, but Monsieur l'Abbé is my invited guest, and . . .' 'He's offended himself by inviting the Abbé and receiving me, and with me so many other good-for-nothings like me . . .' 'Come on, Rameau darling, you must beg the Abbé's pardon . . .' 'What do I want with his pardon!' 'Oh come on, Rameau, it'll all blow over . . .' She takes me by the hand and drags me over to the Abbé's armchair; I stretch my arms out and look at the Abbé with something close to admiration, for who in the world can ever have begged the Abbé's pardon? 'Abbé,' I say, 'this is all quite ridiculous, isn't it? . . .' And then I start to laugh, and so does he. So there I was, pardoned by that party; but the other one still had to be approached, and what I must say to him was a horse of another colour. I can't now recall exactly how I phrased my apology . . . 'Monsieur, I'm a stupid fool . . .' 'I've had to put up with his nonsense for too long; I never want to hear his name mentioned again . . .' 'He's sorry . . .' 'Yes, I'm very sorry . . .' 'He'll never do it again . . .' 'Until the next opportunity . . .' I don't know whether he was in one of those black moods when Mademoiselle daren't go near him or touch him without her velvet gloves, or whether he misheard what I said, or whether I said the wrong thing; but things were worse than before. What the hell, doesn't he know what I am? Doesn't he know that I'm

like a child, that there are occasions when I just let everything
go? And then, God forgive me, can't I have one single moment
to relax? Even a puppet made of steel would be worn out if its
strings were jerked from dawn to dusk and then from dusk to
dawn. I have to keep them entertained; it's the requirement;
but I have to have a bit of fun myself now and again. In the
midst of all this confusion a disastrous thought came into
my head, a thought that made me feel defiant and insolently
proud: the thought that they couldn't do without me, that I
was essential to them.

ME: Yes, I believe you're very useful to them, but they're even
more useful to you. You're not going to find, when you need it,
another house as good; but they—well for every fool they have
to do without, they'll find a hundred others.

HIM: A hundred fools like me! No, Master Philosopher, they're
not that common. Oh, there are plenty of boring fools. But
with foolishness, people are harder to please than with talent,
or virtue. I'm rare among my kind, yes, very rare. Now that
they've no longer got me, however are they managing? They're
as dull as ditchwater. I'm an inexhaustible fountain of impudence. I was never without a sally that made them laugh till
they cried; they saw me as a complete lunatic asylum of their
very own.

ME: And you also had your meals, your bed, your coat, jacket,
breeches, and shoes, and your spending-money every month.

HIM: That was the good side, the profit; but the costs, you've said
nothing about them. First, if rumour spoke of a new play, I was
required, regardless of the weather, to go ferreting through all
the attics in Paris until I'd found the author, succeeded in
reading the work, and adroitly dropped a hint that one of the
parts would be superbly played by an acquaintance of mine . . .
'And who is that, may I ask?' 'Who? What a question! One
who unites all graces, all sweetness, all subtlety . . .' 'You must
mean Mademoiselle Dangeville, do you really know her?'
'Yes, slightly, but she's not the one . . .' 'Who is it then?' I
murmur the name. 'Her!' 'Yes, her,' I would repeat, rather

shamefacedly. For sometimes I do feel ashamed; you should see how the playwright's face would fall on hearing that name repeated; sometimes, he'd just explode with laughter in my face. Nevertheless, I had to get my fellow, willy-nilly, to the dinner table; he, afraid of committing himself, would sulkily refuse. And you should have seen the way I'd be treated if I failed in my mission—called a lout, a blunderer, stupid, utterly useless, not worth the glass of water they allowed me. But it was even worse when she actually got a part, and I had to go and—deaf to the booing of a public whose judgement, contrary to general belief, is good—bravely let my solitary applause ring out, and endure the stares and, sometimes, the hisses that *she* had earned; hear people round me whisper: 'It's a footman in disguise, he belongs to the man she's sleeping with; when *will* the bastard stop that row!' People don't know why someone does what I did; they assume it's out of ineptness, whereas it springs from a motive that excuses everything.

ME: Even contravening the laws of civilized behaviour.

HIM: Eventually I'd be recognized, and they'd say: 'Oh, it's only Rameau.' My solution was to throw in the odd ironic comment that rescued my solitary applause from seeming ridiculous, by making it mean its opposite. You must agree that it takes a powerful incentive to defy the assembled public like that, and that each one of these thankless tasks was worthy of a decent remuneration.

ME: Why didn't you insist on some help?

HIM: Occasionally I did, and made a bit on the side that way. Before entering the torture-chamber, one had to commit to memory all the brilliant bits, where it was so vital to set the right tone. If I happened to forget them and pick the wrong moments, thunderbolts struck me upon my return—you simply can't imagine the hullabaloo. And at home there was a pack of dogs to look after; it's true I'd stupidly taken on this job; and I had charge of the cats—I was lucky if *Micou* didn't claw my hand or tear my cuff! *Criquette* tends to be colicky and I'm the one who massages her belly. In the early days Mademoiselle

54

suffered from the vapours; now, it's nerves, not to mention other slight indispositions that she discusses freely in front of me. That's fine with me: I've never assumed my presence should inhibit anyone. I've read somewhere that at times a king known as *le Grand* liked to lean on the back of his mistress's commode. People tend to ignore decorum when they're with their familiars, and in those days I was more familiar than anyone else. I'm the apostle of familiarity and ease. I preached to them by example, without anyone objecting; they should simply have let me go on like that. I've sketched the *patron* for you. Mademoiselle's beginning to get fat; you should just hear the great stories they're telling about that!

ME: But surely you're not one of those people.

HIM: Why not?

ME: Because at the very least it's bad manners to tell tales that ridicule your benefactors.

HIM: But isn't it even worse to use one's own position as benefactor to vilify one's protégé?

ME: But if the protégé were not vile already, nothing would give the benefactor the power to do that.

HIM: But if the individuals concerned were not themselves already ridiculous, people wouldn't tell those great stories. And then, is it my fault if they keep low company? Is it my fault, if, when they're in that company, they're betrayed and ridiculed? When people choose to live with people like us, if they've any sense, they must be prepared for all manner of low-down tricks. When they take us in, don't they know us for what we are, self-seeking, base, and faithless? If they do know us to be such, all is well. There's a tacit agreement that they'll treat us well, and that sooner or later we'll return evil for the good they've done us. Isn't there such a pact between a man and his monkey or his parrot? Brun complains loudly that Palissot, his guest and friend, has written some couplets attacking him. Palissot had to write the couplets, and it's Brun who's in the wrong. Poinsinet complains loudly that Palissot's attributed to him the couplets he wrote against Brun. Palissot had to attribute to Poinsinet the couplets he wrote against Brun, and it's Poinsinet who's in the wrong. The little Abbé Rey complains loudly because his friend Palissot has pinched his mistress, after Rey himself had taken Palissot to visit her. The point is that he should either not have taken Palissot to see her, or resigned himself to losing her. Palissot did what he had to do, and it's Rey who's in the wrong. The bookseller David loudly complains that his colleague Palissot has slept or tried to sleep with his wife; the bookseller David's wife complains that Palissot's hinting to anyone prepared to believe him that he slept with her; whether Palissot did or did not sleep with the bookseller's wife is a difficult question, since the wife would have to deny it if it did happen, and Palissot may well have insinuated something that did not happen. Whatever the facts of the case, Palissot was faithful to his role, and it's David and his wife who are in the wrong. Helvétius complains loudly that Palissot portrayed him in a play as rude and impolite, when Palissot's still in his debt for medical treatment for his illness, as well as for food and clothing. Should he have expected anything different, from a man tainted by every kind of infamy, who for amusement persuaded his friend to renounce his religion, who steals from his business partners, who has no faith, no moral code, no feelings, who chases money *per fas et nefas*,* whose days are counted out in evil deeds, and who portrayed himself in a play as one of the most dangerous scoundrels ever*—a piece of impudence unrivalled in the past and likely to remain so in the future? No. It's not Palissot, it's Helvétius who's in the wrong. If you take a young man from the provinces to the Versailles menagerie, and he stupidly decides to put his hand between the bars of the tiger's or the panther's cage: if this young man loses his arm in the beast's maw, who is in the wrong? It's all spelled out in the tacit agreement. Hard luck for anyone unaware of that agreement, or who has forgotten it. How often would I not invoke this universal, sacred compact to justify those we accuse of malice, when it is we ourselves and our own stupidity that we should accuse! Yes, my corpulent Countess, it's you who are in the wrong, when you gather round you what your circle calls 'types', and then these 'types' stab you in the back, induce you to behave like them, and expose you to the resentment of decent people. The decent people behave as they must; so do the 'types'. You are wrong to keep company with 'types'. If Bertinhus* had lived quietly and peacefully with his mistress; if, because they were decent people, they'd made decent friends; if they'd gathered round them men of talent, men known in society for their virtues; if they'd reserved for a small, choice, enlightened circle of friends the hours of relaxation they could spare from the pleasure of being together, of loving one another and sharing their feelings at their own quiet fireside, do you suppose that any stories—whether good or bad—would have been made up about them? But what in fact did happen to them? They got what they deserved. They were punished for their imprudence; we are the means appointed for all eternity by Providence to mete out justice to the Bertins of our day, and it is those of our posterity who resemble us that will see justice done to the Monsauges and the Bertins still to come. But while we execute Providence's just decrees on stupidity, you, who depict us as we really are, you execute her just decrees on us. What would you think of us, if, with our shameful way of life, we laid claim to public respect? You would think us mad. And people who expect decent treatment at the hands of those who are innately corrupt, whose characters are vile and base, are they wise? Everything in this world pays its just dues. There are two attorneys-general: one lives amongst us, and punishes offences against society. The other one is Nature. Nature deals with all the vices that escape the law. Abandon yourself to a life of debauchery and womanizing and you'll develop dropsy; if you're profligate and dissolute, your lungs will suffer. Open your door to riff-raff, live with them; you'll be betrayed, ridiculed, scorned. The simplest thing is to resign yourself to the fairness of Nature's judgements, and tell yourself: it's all as it should be; then either pull yourself together and mend your ways, or remain as you are, but accept the aforesaid contract.

ME: You're right.

HIM: And by the way, about those unkind stories, not one of them originates with me; I stick to the part of scandalmonger. It appears that a few days ago, about five in the morning, the most outrageous hullabaloo broke out; all the bells were ringing at once, and broken, muffled cries were heard as of a man being asphyxiated: 'Help, help, I'm suffocating, I'm dying.' These cries came from the *patron*'s room. People rush in and help him. Our fat friend, who'd completely lost her head, and was blind and deaf to everything, as often happens in this situation, went on moving faster and faster, raising herself up on her hands and then, from the highest point she could attain, letting drop upon the Private Parts of the Treasury a two- or three-hundred pound weight, with a momentum energized by the most raging desire. To free him was a Herculean task. But what a crazy notion, for a tiny hammer to place itself beneath a massive anvil!

ME: You're a scoundrel. Let's change the subject. Ever since we began talking, I've been longing to ask you something.

HIM: So why have you waited all this time?

ME: Because I was afraid of presuming.

HIM: After what I've just been saying, I can't think what secrets I haven't already told you.

ME: You're in no doubt about my opinion of your character.

HIM: In none whatever. I'm a very abject, very despicable being in your eyes, and occasionally—albeit rarely—in my own as well. I more often congratulate myself on my vices than castigate myself for them. You're more consistent in your scorn.

ME: True. But why reveal to me all your depravity?

HIM: In the first place, because you were already aware of most of it; and then, I judged I had more to gain than lose by confessing the remainder.

ME: How so, if I may ask?

HIM: If there's any area in which it really matters to be sublime, it is, above all else, in wickedness. People spit upon a petty thief, but cannot refuse a kind of respect to a great criminal.

His courage astounds, his cruelty terrifies. People value unity of character in everything.

ME: But you have not yet developed this prized unity of character. At times you seem to vacillate in your principles. It isn't clear whether your wickedness comes naturally or through study; or whether study has taken you as far as it can.

HIM: I agree; but I've done my best. Didn't I have sufficient modesty to acknowledge beings more perfect than myself? Didn't I tell you, with the deepest admiration, about Bouret? To my mind, Bouret is the greatest man on earth.

ME: But you come directly after Bouret.

HIM: No.

ME: So it's Palissot?

HIM: It's Palissot, but it's not only Palissot.

ME: And who can be worthy of sharing second place with him?

HIM: The renegade of Avignon.

ME: I've never heard of this renegade of Avignon, but he must be a most astonishing man.

HIM: He most certainly is.

ME: I've always taken an interest in the histories of great men.

HIM: Yes, of course. This one lived with a good and decent descendant of the tribe of Abraham, which, as was promised to the father of believers, is equal in number to the number of stars in the sky.*

ME: With a Jew.

HIM: With a Jew. First he had inspired the Jew's compassion, then his benevolence, and finally his complete trust. That's the way it always happens. We rely so much on the effect of our good deeds, that we almost never conceal our secrets from the recipient of our kindnesses. How can we expect ingratitude not to flourish, when we expose man to the temptation of being ungrateful with impunity? This judicious reflection never occurred to our Jew. He therefore admitted to the renegade that he could not, in good conscience, eat pork. You shall see to what advantage a fertile mind could turn this confession. Several months went by, during which our renegade's devoted attentions grew even greater. When he considered that his Jew was deeply affected and won over by his devotion, and felt he had no better friend among all the tribes of Israel, then—and this deserves our admiration—he showed great prudence. He takes his time. He allows the pear to ripen, before he shakes the branch. Too much enthusiasm might spell the ruin of his enterprise. As a general rule, greatness of character comes from a natural balance between several antithetical qualities.

ME: Enough of your ruminations; get on with your story.

HIM: That's not possible. There are days where I have to ruminate. It's a disease that must run its course. Where was I?

ME: On the establishment of a close relationship between the Jew and the renegade.

HIM: So the pear was now ripe . . . but you're not paying attention. What are you thinking about?

ME: I'm thinking about the way your tone varies; sometimes it's high-flown, sometimes familiar and low.

HIM: Can the tone of an imperfect man be uniform? One evening he knocks at his good friend's door with a terrified air, hardly able to speak, his face pale as death, shaking in every limb . . . 'Whatever's the matter?' 'We're done for.' 'What do you mean, done for?' 'Done for, I tell you; there's no escaping it.' 'But explain yourself.' 'Give me a minute, to get over my fright.' 'Yes, yes, take your time,' the Jew said to him, instead of saying, 'You're an unmitigated scoundrel; I don't know what you're going to tell me, but you're a real scoundrel, your terror's just a sham.'

ME: But why should he speak to him like that?

HIM: Because he was faking, and he'd overstepped the mark. It's clear to me; don't interrupt me again. 'We're done for, there's no hope for us.' Don't you sense the affectation of those repeated *done fors*? 'A traitor's betrayed us to the Holy Inquisition, you as a Jew, I as a renegade, an infamous renegade.' Just listen to the way that traitor unblushingly uses the most odious language. It takes more courage than you might suppose to call oneself by one's true name. You don't know what it takes to reach that point.

ME: I certainly don't. But this infamous renegade . . .

HIM: Was lying; but it was a very clever lie. The Jew is very frightened, tugs at his beard, flings himself about. He imagines the police at his door, sees himself wrapped up in a *san-benito*, his auto-da-fé set up in readiness . . .* 'My dear, my loving friend, my only friend, what should we do?' 'What should we do? Show ourselves, appear perfectly secure, behave as we always do. This tribunal operates in secret, but slowly. This delay must be used to sell off everything. I'll go and charter a vessel—or arrange for someone else to do that; yes, chartering it through someone else would be best. We'll store your fortune aboard; because it's your fortune they're mainly after; and you and I will leave, and seek on some other shore the freedom and security to serve our God and obey the Law of Abraham and of our conscience. What's absolutely vital in this dangerous situation, is not to make a rash move.' No sooner said than done. The ship's chartered, and supplied with provisions and sailors. The Jew's fortune is on board. Tomorrow at dawn they'll set sail. They can dine light-heartedly and sleep securely. Tomorrow they'll escape their persecutors. During the night the renegade gets up, robs the Jew of his wallet, purse, and jewels, boards the vessel, and away he sails. And you think that's the end of it? Ha! You haven't understood. When I was told this tale, I, Rameau, guessed what I've kept from you, to test your shrewdness. You were right to be an honest man, you'd never have been more than a scamp. Up to this point, the renegade is just that. He's a despicable rascal whom no one would choose to emulate. The sublime part of his wickedness is this: he himself had denounced to the Holy Inquisition his good friend the Israelite, who was arrested the next morning, and, a few days later, fuelled a fine bonfire. And that's how the renegade became the tranquil possessor of the fortune of that accursed descendant of those who crucified our Lord.

ME: I don't know which of the two horrifies me more: the villainy of your renegade, or the tone in which you speak of it.

HIM: And that's what I was telling you. The atrocity of the act carries you beyond contempt, and that's why I'm being sincere. I wanted you to realize just how much I excel at my art; force you to admit that I was at least original in my degradation, lay claim, in your thoughts, to my place in the great tradition of super-scoundrels, so that then I can exclaim: *Vivat Mascarillus, fourbum imperator!** Come on, Master Philosopher, let's be merry, all together please: *Vivat Mascarillus, fourbum imperator!*

Whereupon he began an extraordinary fugue-like song. At times the melody would be grave and majestic, at times light-hearted and playful; now he'd be imitating the bass, now a treble part; he'd indicate, by outstretched arm and neck, where the notes were sustained; he performed and composed a song of triumph in his own honour, demonstrating that he knew more about good music than good morals.

For my own part, I couldn't decide whether to stay or leave, laugh or be angry. I stayed, intending to shift the conversation onto some subject that would cleanse my soul of the horror filling it. I was beginning to find it hard to tolerate the presence of a man who could discuss a horrible deed, an abominable, heinous crime, the way a connoisseur of painting or poetry discusses the beauties of a fine work of art, or the way a moralist or a historian points out and emphasizes every aspect of a heroic action. In spite of myself, I was overcome with depression. Observing this, he enquired:

HIM: What's the matter? Are you feeling unwell?

ME: A little, but it'll pass.

HIM: You look anxious, as if you're worrying over some disturbing idea.

ME: That's so.

After a moment's silence on his part as on mine, during which he paced up and down whistling and humming, I said, to bring him back to the subject of his talent: 'What are you doing now?'

HIM: Nothing.

ME: That's most exhausting.

HIM: As it was, I was feeling quite stupid enough already, then I went to hear the music of Duni and our other young composers and that really finished me.

ME: So you approve of that style of music?

HIM: Definitely.

ME: And to your ear these new melodies sound beautiful?

HIM: Do they sound beautiful! My goodness! A thousand times yes. Such declamation! Such truth! Such feeling!

ME: All imitative art takes its models from nature. What is the model the musician uses in composing a melody?

HIM: Why not start at the beginning? What is a melody?

ME: That question, I admit, is beyond me. We're all the same. Our memories contain only words which, from the frequent and even the appropriate use we make of them, we believe we understand, and our minds contain only vague notions. When I utter the word 'melody', I have no clearer idea in my mind than do you and most of your fellow men when they say 'reputation, blame, honour, vice, virtue, modesty, decency, shame, ridicule'.

HIM: Melody is an imitation, using the notes of a scale invented by art or copied from nature (you decide), with the human voice or an instrument as its medium, that mimics physical sounds or tones of passion; and, as you can see, by changing the necessary terms in that definition it would precisely fit painting, eloquence, sculpture, and poetry. Now, as to your question. What's the model for the musician or melody? It's declamation, if the model breathes and thinks, sound, if the model's inanimate. Declamation should be pictured as a line, and melody as another line that snakes up and down above it. The more powerful and true the declamation—the model for the song—the more the song mirroring it will break it into

63

separate phrases; then the truer the song, and the more beautiful. And that's what our young musicians have understood so
well. When you hear: 'I'm a poor devil', you feel you're listening to a miser's lament; if he weren't singing, he'd be using that
same tone to say, as he entrusts his gold to the earth: 'Oh earth,
receive my treasure'.* And that young girl who feels her heart
beating rapidly and, blushing, flustered, begs *monseigneur* to
permit her to leave, would she express herself otherwise? These
works present a great variety of characters and a wide range of
declamatory styles. They're sublime, I tell you. Go and listen,
please, listen to the piece where the dying youth cries out: 'My
heart's forsaking me'.* Listen to the song; listen to the accompaniment, and afterwards tell me in what way the actual tones
of the dying man, and the form of this melody, differ. You'll see
if the modulations of the melody do not perfectly coincide with
those of the spoken word. I'm saying nothing about the metre,
which is another essential component of melody; I'm only concerned with the expression; nothing could be more self-evident
than this maxim, which I read somewhere: *musices seminarium
accentus*: metre is the source of melody.* From which you can
see how difficult, and how essential, it is to know how to perform recitative properly. There's no beautiful melody which
cannot be made into a beautiful recitative, and no beautiful
recitative from which a clever musician cannot create a beautiful melody. I'd hesitate to assert that someone who declaims
well would sing well, but I'd be surprised if a fine singer
weren't good at declamation. You must believe all this that I'm
telling you, for it's the truth.

ME: There's nothing I'd like better than to believe you, if I were
not prevented by a trifling difficulty.

HIM: Which is?

ME: If this music is sublime, then it follows that the music of the
divine Lully, of Campra, of Destouches, of Mouret and even—
just between you and me—even that of the dear uncle must be
a bit dull.

HIM [coming right up to me and murmuring his reply in my

ear]: I don't want to be overheard, for there are plenty of
people here who know me; but the fact is, it *is* dull. It's not that
I'm worried about the dear uncle—since 'dear' is what we're
calling him. He's made of stone. He'd see me with my tongue
hanging out a foot from my mouth and wouldn't give me a
glass of water. But however hard he tries—with octaves, with
sevenths (tum, tum, tatata, tirelee, tirelee, da) making the devil
of a din, those who're beginning to see through him, and no
longer confuse a tremendous racket with music, won't ever
come to terms with it. There should be a police order forbid-
ding anyone, regardless of their rank or position, from having
Pergolesi's *Stabat Mater* sung. That *Stabat* ought to have been
burnt by the public executioner. My goodness, those damned
Italian *bouffons*, with their *Serva padrona* and their *Tracollo*,
have really given us a good kick in the pants.* In the old days a
Tancrède, an *Issé*, a *Europe galante*, *Les Indes*, *Castor*, *Les Talents
lyriques* played for four, five, six months. An *Armide* ran forever.* These days, they keep coming one after the other, falling
like ninepins. So Rebel and Francœur* are foaming at the
mouth. They're saying they're done for; ruined; and that if
people put up with those trashy fairground music-makers any
longer, the national music will go to the devil, and that the
Académie Royale, down in the back alley*—the Opéra—might
as well put up its shutters. And they do have a point. The old
fossils who've been going there every Friday for thirty or forty
years no longer find it as much fun as they did in the past;
they're bored and they nod off without knowing why; they
wonder about it, but can't come up with an explanation. Why
don't they ask me? Duni's prediction will come true, and the
way things are going, I'd stake my life that within four or five
years of the *Peintre amoureux de son modèle*,* you won't see a
living soul in the famous alley. Those simple souls, they've
deserted their own symphonies for the Italian ones. They
imagined their ears would become attuned to the latter without
it affecting their vocal music, as if a symphony were not,
in relation to song—allowing always for the range of the

instrument and the dexterity of the fingers—what song is in relation to actual declamation. As if the violin were not the ape of the singer, who'll one day become, when complexity's replaced beauty, the ape of the violin. The first musician to perform Locatelli was the apostle of the new music. There'll be others, many others. We'll grow accustomed to imitations of the accents of passion or the phenomena of nature, through melody, voice, and instruments, for that's the real range of the purpose of music. Do you then suppose that we'll keep our taste for pillage, spears, triumphal marches, ovations, victory celebrations? 'Go and see if they're coming, Jean.'* They'd imagined the public would weep or laugh at tragic or comic scenes that had been transmuted into music; that they could let the public hear tones of rage, hatred, and jealousy, genuine love laments, and the ironies and jokes of the Italian or French theatre, and that they'd still admire *Ragonde* and *Platée*.* My reply to that is: fiddle-faddle. They'd imagined that they could regularly let the public experience with what ease, flexibility, and fluidity the harmony and metre of the Italian tongue, with its ellipses and inversions, adapt themselves to the art, movement, expression, and structure of the songs and the measured rhythm of the sounds, and that they'd still fail to notice how stiff, hollow, heavy, unwieldy, pedantic, and monotonous is their own tongue.* But such is the case. They've told themselves that the public, after mingling its tears with the tears of a mother bewailing the death of her son, after shuddering at a tyrant's murderous decree, wouldn't be bored by their fairyland decors, their insipid mythology, their mawkish little madrigals which reveal as much about the poet's bad taste as they do about the sterility of the art that tolerates them. The simple souls! It is not so, and never will be. The rights of the true, the good, and the beautiful will always prevail. They may be contested, but in the long run they're admired. Art lacking in these qualities may be admired for a time, but eventually the applause gives way to yawns. So yawn away, my friends, yawn to your hearts' content. Don't be embarrassed. The supremacy of nature and of my trinity is such that the forces of hell can never prevail against it—Truth which is the Father, engendering Good, which is the Son, whence comes Beauty, which is the Holy Spirit—my trinity establishes its dominion imperceptibly. The foreign god humbly takes his place upon the altar, at the side of the indigenous idol; little by little he consolidates his position until, one fine day, he gives his neighbour a gentle shove; and—lo and behold! the idol falls. It's said that that's how the Jesuits introduced Christianity into China and India. And whatever those Jansenists may say, this political system that makes straight for its target without commotion, or bloodshed, or martyrs, without hurting a hair of anybody's head, strikes me as the best.

ME: There's good sense—or something like it—in everything you've been saying.

HIM: Sense! That's fortunate. Devil take me if I'm trying to make sense. I say whatever comes into my mind. I'm like the Opéra musicians when my uncle first appeared: if I'm doing it right, so much the better. After all, an apprentice coalman will always speak more pertinently of his trade than would an entire academy or all the Duhamels in the world.

Whereupon he began pacing up and down, quietly humming some of the melodies from *L'Isle des Fous*, *Le Peintre amoureux de son modèle*, *Le Maréchal ferrant*, and *La Plaideuse*.* From time to time, raising his hands, he'd gaze up at the sky and exclaim: 'My God, isn't that beautiful, isn't that beautiful! How could anyone possessing a pair of ears even ask such a question?' Next he started working himself into a passion. He was singing softly, and as his excitement increased his voice grew louder; then he began gesturing, grimacing, and twisting about. I said to myself: 'Right, now he's about to lose his head, and there'll be another scene.' And indeed, he suddenly shouted: '*I am a worthless wretch . . . my lord. My lord, permit me to depart . . . oh earth, receive my gold; guard my treasure well . . . my soul, my soul, my life! Oh earth! . . . my dear friend is here . . . he's here! . . . aspettare e non venire . . . a*

Zerbina penserete . . . sempre in contrasti con te si sta . . .'* Now he
was muddling and mixing some thirty airs of every style—Italian,
French, tragic, comic; sometimes, singing a bass part, he'd des-
cend into the depths of hell; sometimes, straining at the notes as
he imitated a falsetto, he'd tear at the upper registers, all the while
imitating, with gait, carriage, and gestures, the different characters singing; by turns furious, mollified, imperious, derisive.
Now he's a young girl in tears, mimicking all her simpering ways;
now he's a priest, a king, a tyrant, threatening, commanding,
raging; now he's a slave, obeying. He grows calmer, he grieves, he
laments, he laughs; never does he misjudge the tone, pace, and
meaning of the aria's words and character. All the chess players
had abandoned their games and gathered round him. Outside,
the windows of the café were thronged with passers-by attracted
by the noise. The roars of laughter were loud enough to open
cracks in the ceiling. He noticed nothing of this; he just went on
with his performance, transported by a passion, an enthusiasm so
akin to madness that it wasn't clear whether he'd ever recover
from it, or whether he shouldn't be flung into a carriage and taken
straight to the madhouse, still singing a fragment from Jommelli's
Lamentations. He was performing the most beautiful passages of
each work with incredible fidelity, sincerity, and warmth: the
exquisite, fully orchestrated recitative where the prophet depicts
the devastation of Jerusalem he accompanied with a torrent of
tears, which drew further tears from the eyes of all the onlookers.
Everything was there—the delicacy of the melody, the intensity
of expression, and the pain. He stressed the moments where the
composer had shown himself to be a particularly fine master of
his art; if he abandoned the vocal part, it was to take up the
instruments, which he'd suddenly drop to return to the voice;
connecting one with the other in such a fashion as to preserve the
links and the unity of the whole; taking possession of our souls
and keeping them suspended in the most extraordinary state of
being I have ever known . . . Was I filled with admiration? Yes, I
was. Was I moved to pity? Yes, I was; but a tinge of ridicule was
blended with these feelings, and denatured them.

You'd have burst out laughing, seeing how he imitated the various instruments. The horns and bassoons he did with bulging, ballooning cheeks and a hoarse, mournful tone; for the oboes he adopted a piercing, nasal sound; he speeded up his voice to an unbelievable pace for the stringed instruments, seeking the truest sounds; the piccolos he whistled; the transverse flutes he warbled; shouting, singing, flinging himself about like a madman, being, just he alone, at once dancer and ballerina, tenor and soprano, the entire orchestra, the entire theatre, dividing himself into twenty different roles, running and then stopping, with the air of one possessed, eyes flashing, lips foaming. The heat was overpowering; the sweat, mingled with the powder from his hair, was streaming along the creases of his brow and down his cheeks, and flowing in channels over the upper part of his coat. Was there anything I didn't see him do? He wept, he laughed, he sighed; he gazed tenderly, or placidly, or furiously; he was a woman swooning with grief; a wretch overcome with despair; a temple rising up from the ground; birds falling silent at sunset; rivers murmuring their way through cool solitudes or cascading down from high mountains; a storm; a tempest, the moans of the dying mingling with the whistling of the wind and the crashing of the thunder; night, with its darkness; shadows and silence—for sound can portray silence itself. He had completely lost touch with reality. Utterly spent, like someone emerging from a deep sleep or a long trance, he stood there motionless, stupefied, astounded. He gazed all around, as would a man who had mistaken his way and was trying to discover where he was. As he waited for his strength and his wits to return, he kept automatically wiping his face. Like a man who, on waking, finds his bed surrounded by a large number of people, but has not the faintest recollection of what he's been doing, he immediately exclaimed: 'Well, gentlemen, what's the matter? Why are you laughing, why are you so surprised, what is it?' Then he added: 'Now that's what's meant by the words music and musician. However, gentlemen, we shouldn't despise some of Lully's pieces. I challenge anyone to compose anything better than the music of 'Ah, j'attendrai',* without changing the words.

We shouldn't despise certain passages in Campra, my uncle's violin melodies, his gavottes; his processions of soldiers, clergy, high priests . . . "*Pale torches, night more ghastly than the shadowy dark . . . Gods of Tartarus, and of oblivion . . .*" '* Here his voice swelled, sustaining the notes; neighbours came to their windows and we stuck our fingers in our ears. He added: 'Here's where good lungs are required, a mighty voice, plenty of air. But soon, it'll be goodbye to the feast of the Assumption; Lent and the Kings are over. As yet they don't know what should be put to music, nor, consequently, what suits the musician. We still await the birth of lyric poetry. But they'll get there, by dint of hearing Pergolesi, Hasse, Terradeglias, Traetta, and the others, by dint of reading Metastasio, they surely must get there.'

ME: What are you saying, that Quinault, La Motte, Fontenelle didn't know how to write?

HIM: Not for the new style of music. There aren't six consecutive lines in all their charming poems that can be set to music. They give us ingenious maxims and light, tender, delicate madrigals; but if you want to discover how lacking they are in material suited to our art, which is the most violent of all arts, not even excepting that of Demosthenes, have someone recite these pieces to you; how cold, vapid, monotonous they'll seem! That's because there's nothing in them to supply a model for song. I'd sooner have to set to music La Rochefoucauld's *Maximes* or Pascal's *Pensées*.* The animal cry of passion should be what determines the melodic line. Expressions of passion should come fast one upon another; they should be brief and their meaning fragmented, suspenseful, so that the musician can use the whole as well as each part, omit a word or repeat it, add a word that's missing, turn the phrase upside-down and inside-out like a polyp, without destroying its meaning; this makes French lyrical poetry much more difficult to set to music than poetry in languages with inversion, which provide all these advantages naturally . . . *Plunge your dagger in my breast, cruel barbarian. I am ready to receive the fatal blow. Strike,*

dare to strike . . . ah, I faint, I die . . . a secret fire inflames my
senses . . . cruel love, what do you ask of me . . . Leave me with the
sweet peace I used to know . . . give me back my reason . . . The
passions must be intense and the sensibility of the musician
and lyric poet extreme. Almost always, the aria is the culminat-
ing point of the scene: we need exclamations, interjections,
pauses, interruptions, affirmations, denials; we call out, invoke,
shout, moan, weep, laugh openly. No wit, no epigrams, none
of those pretty conceits. They're too remote from simple
nature. And don't imagine that the theatrical style of acting
and declamation can serve us as a model. What an idea! We
need it to be more energetic, less mannered, truer. Simple
speech, the common words of passion, we need these all the
more where the language is more monotone, less accented.
The animal cry—the cry of man in a passion—will give it the
accent it lacks.

While he was talking to me in this way the crowd surrounding us
had dissipated, either because it didn't understand, or because it
took no interest in his remarks, for as a rule children, like men,
and men, like children, would sooner be amused than instructed.
The chess players had resumed their games, and we were left
alone in our corner. Seated on a bench, his head leaning against
the wall, his eyes half closed and his arms dangling, he said to me:
'I don't know what's the matter with me, when I came I felt fresh
as a daisy, and now I'm worn out, exhausted, as if I'd walked for
miles and miles. It hit me quite suddenly.'

ME: Would you like something to drink?

HIM: Yes, very much. I feel hoarse, and weak; my chest hurts a
bit. This happens to me almost every day, just like that, I don't
know why.

ME: What would you like?

HIM: Whatever you think. I'm not particular. Poverty's taught
me to like anything.

They serve us beer and lemonade. He pours some into a big glass which he empties two or three times in quick succession. Then, like a man restored to life, he gives a tremendous cough, shifts about in his seat, and goes on: 'But in your opinion, Master Philosopher, isn't it extremely odd that a foreigner, an Italian, a Duni, should come and teach us how to accentuate our music, and adapt our songs to all the tempi, metres, intervals, declamatory passages, without harming prosody? After all, it wasn't all that difficult a thing to do. Anyone who'd heard a down-and-out begging in the street, a man in the grip of rage, a jealous, furious woman, a lover in despair, a flatterer—yes, a flatterer softening his tone, drawling out his syllables, his voice like honey; in a word, a passion, no matter what kind, provided that by its intensity it deserved to serve as a model for the musician, must have noticed two things: first, that syllables, whether long or short, have no fixed duration, and are not even in any necessary proportional relationship to each other; second, that passion can mould prosody more or less at will; it accommodates the very longest intervals, and the man who cries out in deep despair: "*Ah! Wretched that I am!*" raises his voice on the first exclamatory syllable to the highest, sharpest pitch and sinks down on the others to the gravest and lowest, ranging over an octave or even more and giving each sound the quantity appropriate to the melody, without offending the ear or letting the syllables, be they long or short, preserve the length or brevity of unemotional speech. We've come a long way since the days when we would cite, as miracles of musical expression, the parenthetical remark in *Armide*: "Rinaldo's conqueror (if any such exists)", or "Let us not hesitate, but obey!" from *Les Indes galantes*.* Now, those miracles make me shrug my shoulders with pity. The rate at which the art is moving ahead, no one can predict where it'll get to. While we're waiting, let's have a drink.'

He had two, then three, without noticing what he was doing. He would surely have drowned himself, the same way he'd exhausted himself, without realizing it if I hadn't pushed away the bottle, which he kept reaching for absent-mindedly. **Then I** said to him:

ME: How can it be that with such delicacy of feeling, such great sensitivity towards the beauties of musical art, you're so blind to the beauties of morality, so insensible to the charms of virtue?

HIM: Apparently some people have a sense that's missing in me, a fibre I wasn't granted, or a loose string that it's useless to pluck because it doesn't vibrate; or perhaps it's because I've always lived with good musicians and bad people, which is why my ear has become very acute and my heart very deaf. And then there's the question of heredity. My father's blood and my uncle's is the same blood. My blood's the same as my father's. The paternal molecule was hard and obtuse, and that accursed original molecule's taken over all the others.

ME: Do you love your child?

HIM: Do I love him, the little savage? I'm crazy about him.

ME: And won't you do your utmost to halt the effect on him of the accursed paternal molecule?

HIM: Trying to do that would be, I believe, absolutely useless. If he's destined to be a good man, I won't do him any harm. But if the molecule drove him to be a ne'er-do-well like his father, any attempts of mine to make him into an honest man would harm him greatly; his education would be perpetually at odds with the influence of the molecule, he'd be pulled by two contrary forces and would travel the path of life all askew, like countless people I see who are equally inept in good and in evil; they're what we call 'types', of all epithets the most to be feared, because it indicates mediocrity, and the ultimate in contempt. A great scoundrel is a great scoundrel, he's not a 'type'. It would take forever for the paternal molecule to regain control, and draw him into the state of utter degradation that I've attained; he'd have wasted his best years. So for now I'm leaving him alone. I'm letting him develop. I observe him. He's already greedy, glib, rascally, lazy, lying. I'm very much afraid his pedigree's beginning to show.

ME: And will you make him a musician, so that the likeness is perfect?

HIM: A musician! A musician! Sometimes I look at him and say, grinding my teeth: 'If ever you were to learn one note, I do believe I'd wring your neck!'

ME: Why so, may I ask?

HIM: It doesn't lead to anything.

ME: It leads to everything.

HIM: Yes, when you excel; but who can guarantee that his child's going to excel? It's ten thousand to one that he'll be nothing but a wretched fiddle-scraper like me. Do you know that it may be easier to find a child fit to govern a kingdom, to be a great king, than to be a great violinist?

ME: It seems to me that pleasing talents, even when they're mediocre, can rapidly advance a man on the road to fortune, in a country without morals that's given up to profligacy and luxury. I myself once heard the following conversation, which took place between a couple we'll call patron and protégé. The latter had been referred to the former, as to someone well disposed who might be of service to him . . . 'Monsieur, what are you good at?' 'I'm quite a good mathematician.' 'Well then, teach mathematics; after you've spent ten or twelve years pounding Paris's muddy pavements, you'll be earning three or four hundred francs a year.' 'I've studied law, I know it thoroughly . . .' 'If Pufendorf and Grotius came back to earth, they'd starve to death in the street.' 'I'm well versed in history and geography . . .' 'If there were any parents who really cared about their children's education, your fortune would be made, but there aren't any . . .' 'I'm a good musician . . .' 'Well, why didn't you say so at once! And to show you how valuable this last talent is, listen, I've a daughter. Come every day from seven-thirty till nine in the evening, you'll give her a lesson and I'll give you six hundred francs a year. You'll breakfast and dine and sup with us. The remainder of the day will be yours to use to your advantage.'

HIM: And what happened to this man?

ME: Had he been wise he'd have made his fortune, the only thing, apparently, that matters to you.

HIM: Absolutely. Gold, gold. Gold is everything; the rest, without gold, is nothing. Therefore, instead of stuffing his head with fine precepts that he'll have to forget, or risk being a pauper, I do this: whenever I have a golden louis—which doesn't happen to me often—I plant myself in front of him. I take the louis out of my pocket. I show it to him admiringly. I raise my eyes to heaven. I kiss the louis in front of him. And to make him understand even better the importance of the sacred coin, I stammer as I name and point to everything it can buy, a beautiful gown for a child, a beautiful little cap, a fine cake. Next I put the gold coin in my pocket, I strut proudly about, I pull aside my coat-tail and tap my fingers on my pocket; and that's how I make him understand that the self-confidence he sees in me comes from the louis in my possession.

ME: No one could do better. But what if he, having thoroughly grasped the value of that louis, were one day to . . .

HE: I take your meaning. One must shut one's eyes to such things. There's no moral principle that doesn't have its drawback. At worst, it's a nasty interlude, but then it's over and done with.

ME: Even after hearing such brave, wise views, I still think it would be a good thing to make a musician of him. I know of no better way of rapidly gaining access to those with power, of serving their vices, and turning one's own to good account.

HE: That's true; but I've plans for a quicker, surer path to success. Ah, if only he'd been a girl! But since we can't always have what we'd like, we must be satisfied with what comes and do our best with it; which means not being as foolish as are the majority of fathers, who (and they couldn't do worse if they'd actually planned to make their son's life miserable) give a Spartan-style education to a child destined to live in Paris. If the education he receives is bad, the moral standards of this nation are to blame, not I. Who knows where the responsibility

75

lies. I want my son to be happy or, which amounts to the same thing, respected, rich, and powerful. I know something about the easiest ways to achieve this end, and I'll instruct him therein early in life. If you and your wise friends blame me, the masses, and his success, will absolve me. He'll have his gold— you can take my word for it. If he has a great deal, he'll lack for nothing, not even your good opinion and your respect.

ME: You could be wrong there.

HIM: Or he can manage without them, like many others.

There was, in what he was saying, much that we all think, and by which we guide our behaviour, but do not actually say. In truth, this was the most striking difference between my man and the majority of other people. He admitted to the vices that he, in common with others, had; but he was not a hypocrite. He was neither more nor less odious than they were, he was simply franker, more consistent, and occasionally profound in his depravity. I trembled at what his child might become under such a master. It was clear that under a regime of education so carefully calculated to suit our mores, he should go far, unless his way was prematurely cut short.

HIM: Don't worry! The important point, the difficult point to which a father must pay particular attention, is not to give his child vices which would enrich him, or ridiculous habits which would endear him to those in power; that's what everyone does, although not systematically like me, but at any rate by example and precept; no, instead he must teach him moderation and restraint, and the art of eluding disgrace, dishonour, and the law. Those are discords in social harmony which one must know how to time, prepare and resolve. There's nothing as boring as a succession of harmonious chords. What's wanted is an irritant, something to break up the light and scatter its rays.

ME: Excellent. Your comparison brings me from mores back to music, which I had left unwillingly, and I thank you; for, to be quite frank, I like you better as a musician than as a moralist.

HIM: Nevertheless I'm quite mediocre as a musician, and as a moralist I'm second to none.

ME: I doubt that; but even supposing it to be the case, I'm a simple honest man and your principles aren't mine.

HIM: So much the worse for you. Ah, if only I had your talents.

ME: Let's leave my talents alone, and get back to yours.

HIM: If only I could express myself like you. But I've a damnably absurd kind of style, half high–class and literary, half from the gutter.

ME: I don't speak well. All I can do is tell the truth, and, as you know, that's not always welcome.

HIM: But it's not in order to tell the truth that I covet your talent; no, quite the reverse, it's in order to tell lies well. If only I knew how to write, how to fling a book together, embroider a dedication, turn some fool's head with praise, and insinuate myself with women!

ME: But you're a thousand times better at doing all those things than I am. I'm not even fit to be your pupil.

HIM: How many great qualities you've let go to waste, without even realizing their value!

ME: I reap all that I sow.

HIM: If that were true, you wouldn't be wearing that coat and waistcoat of coarse cloth, those woollen hose and thick-soled shoes, nor that ancient wig.

ME: I agree. A man must be truly inept if he's not rich, while permitting himself every latitude in order to become so. But the fact is, there are people like me who don't value riches as the most precious thing on earth; strange people.

HIM: Very strange. People aren't born like that. They become like that, for it isn't to be found in nature.

ME: Not in man's nature?

HIM: Not in man's nature. Everything that lives, not excepting man, seeks the good things of life for himself, at the expense of those who already possess them. I'm convinced that if I were to let the little savage grow up without telling him anything, he'd want to be handsomely dressed, superbly fed, popular with

77

men and loved by women, and possessed of every blessing life has to offer.

ME: If your little savage were left to fend for himself, if he kept all his natural artlessness and then united the minimal reasoning power of an infant with the violent passions of a man of thirty, he'd strangle his father and bed his mother.

HIM: Which proves that a good education is indispensable—and who's saying otherwise? And what's a good education, if not one which leads, without danger or inconvenience, to every kind of enjoyment?

ME: I almost agree with you, but we'd better not go into details.

HIM: Why not?

ME: Because I'm afraid we're only superficially in agreement, and if once we start discussing the dangers and inconveniences to avoid, we'll find that we no longer think alike.

HIM: And why would that matter?

ME: Let's leave it, I say. What I know on the subject I would not be able to teach you; you could more easily teach me what you know about music but I don't. My dear Rameau, let's talk about music, and tell me how it's come about that with your gift of experiencing, remembering, and reproducing the most beautiful passages from the great masters, with the passion they inspire in you and you convey to others, you yourself haven't created anything worthwhile.

Instead of answering me, he began nodding his head, and, pointing his finger at the sky, then he went on: 'My star, my star! When nature fashioned Leo, Vinci, Pergolesi, Duni, she smiled. She assumed a serious, imposing air when she made my dear uncle Rameau, who was called "the great Rameau" for a decade or so, and who will soon never be mentioned again. When she flung together the nephew, she pulled a face, and then another face, and then yet another'; and as he said this he was making all sorts of faces that expressed scorn, disdain, irony; and he seemed to be kneading a bit of dough between his fingers and grinning at the ridiculous shapes he was giving to it. This done, he tossed the freakish little figurine far away, remarking: 'That's how she made me and threw me down alongside other porcelain figurines, some with huge wrinkled bellies, short necks, and big, bulging, apoplectic eyes; others with crooked necks; some were dried up, with bright eyes and hooked noses; they all burst out laughing on seeing me, just as I clutched my sides and burst out laughing on seeing them; for fools and madmen amuse each other; they seek one another out, they're drawn to one another. Had I not found, upon arriving there, the proverb already coined that goes: "a fool's purse is the patrimony of the man with wits," I'd have claimed it as mine by rights. I felt that nature had put what was my rightful inheritance in the purses of the figurines, and I've invented a thousand ways of getting it back.'

ME: I know those ways, you've told me all about them, and I've expressed my deep admiration. But, with such a wide choice of possibilities, why didn't you try your hand at creating something beautiful?

HIM: Here's what a man of the world remarked to Abbé Le Blanc ... The Abbé was saying: 'The Marquise of Pompadour takes me by the hand, leads me to the door of the Académie, and then withdraws her hand. I fall and break both legs.' The man of the world answered: 'Well, Abbé, you have to get up and batter down the door with your head ...' The Abbé replied: 'That's what I tried, and do you know what I got for my trouble? A big bump on my forehead.'

After relating this little tale, my friend began to walk about with his head bent, his air pensive and downcast; he kept sighing, weeping, and lamenting, with hands and eyes raised to the sky, banging his head with his fist hard enough to damage both forehead and fist; then he added: 'It seems to me there is something in there, but however hard I knock and shake, nothing comes out.' Next he began shaking his head and banging his forehead even harder, saying: 'Either nobody's home, or they don't want to answer.'

A moment later, proudly holding his head high and placing his right hand upon his heart, he declared as he strode up and down: 'I can feel, yes, I can feel.' Next he mimicked a man growing angry, indignant, emotional, then a man commanding, then entreating; he began declaiming impromptu speeches full of rage, or commiseration, or loathing, or love; his sketches of the nature of the passions were astonishingly delicate and true. Then he added: 'That's the way, I think. It's coming, now; that's what it means to find a midwife who's able to stimulate, bring on the pains, and make the baby come out. If I'm alone, I take up my pen, I try to write. I gnaw my nails, I rub at my forehead. Nothing doing. Good-night. The god's not at home. I'd convinced myself that I had genius; at the end of the first line I read that I'm a fool, a fool, a fool. But how are you to feel, to soar, to think, to depict vividly, when you keep company with people like those you need to survive, and you live amidst their chatter, the stuff you hear, all that gossip. "It was quite delightful today, out on the boulevard.* Have you seen that actress who does the little chimney-sweep?* She plays it enchantingly." "Monsieur Such-and-such had the finest pair of dapple-greys you could ever hope to see." "The beautiful Madame So-and-so's beginning to go off. Whoever heard of a forty-five-year-old doing her hair like that!" "Young Mademoiselle X is dripping with diamonds that didn't cost her a lot . . ." "You mean that they did cost her a lot . . ." "No, indeed, they did not . . ." "Where did you see her?" "At *L'Enfant d'Arlequin perdu et retrouvé* . . .* They played the despair scene better than it's ever been done. The Punchinello* has a voice, but no subtlety, no soul." "Madame Y has given birth to two babies at once. Each father will have his own . . ." And do you suppose that remarks like that, repeated over and over again every day, inspire and lead to great thoughts?'

ME: No, it would be better to sequester yourself in a garret, live on dry bread and water, and attempt to know yourself.

HIM: Perhaps, but I haven't the courage; and then, to sacrifice one's happiness for a doubtful outcome! And what about the name I bear? Rameau! Being called Rameau, well, it's embarrassing. It doesn't work with talent the way it does with nobility, which passes on, becoming more illustrious as it goes from grandfather to father, from father to son, from son to grandson, without the first generation imposing any particular ability on the descendants. The old stock branches out into a vast tree of fools, but who cares? It's not the same with talent. To deserve even the fame of the father, you have to be cleverer than he. You have to have inherited his fibre. I lack his fibre; but the wrist is supple, the bow plays, and the pot boils. It isn't glory, but it is soup in the pot.

ME: If I were in your shoes I wouldn't settle for that; I'd try.

HIM: And you suppose I haven't done so? I wasn't yet fifteen when I first said to myself: What's the matter, Rameau? You're dreaming. And what are you dreaming of? That you'd love to achieve or to have achieved something the whole world would admire. Ah, yes; all you have to do is whistle and wiggle your fingers. Just say one, two, three, and lo! it's done. As a grown man, I repeated what I'd said as a child. Today I'm still repeating it, and I stay close to Memnon's statue.

ME: Memnon's statue—what are you talking about?

HIM: I think it's obvious. Round Memnon's statue* there were many, many other statues and, like him, they were all standing in a ray of sunlight; but his was the only one that reverberated. Name a poet: Voltaire. And who else? Voltaire. A third? Voltaire. A fourth? Voltaire again. As for musicians, there's Rinaldo of Capua, Hasse, Pergolesi, Alberti, Tartini, Locatelli, Terradeglias, and my uncle; there's that little Duni who has neither looks nor presence but who can feel, by God, and who's a master of melody and expression. The rest of them, hanging about near that small number of Memnons, they're so many pairs of ears stuck on the end of a baton. So we're all dirt-poor, so poor it's like a blessing. Ah, Master Philosopher, poverty's a terrible thing. I see her crouching, open-mouthed, waiting to catch a few drops of icy water that drip from the cask of the Danaides.* I don't know whether poverty sharpens the philosopher's wits, but it's damnably numbing to the mind of a poet. You can't sing well under that cask. You're very lucky if you can find shelter under it. I did, but I wasn't able to stay there. I'd already made the same stupid mistake once before. I've travelled in Bohemia, Germany, Switzerland, Holland, Flanders, to hell and back, God knows where.

ME: Under the leaky cask?

HIM: Under the leaky cask. He was a wealthy, spendthrift Jew who loved music, and my antics. I played music whenever God decreed; I played the fool; I wanted for nothing. My Jew was a man well versed in the law, which he observed punctiliously; almost always when dealing with friends, but with strangers, always. He got into a bad business that I must tell you about; it'll amuse you. There was in Utrecht a charming courtesan. Finding the Christian woman greatly to his taste, he sent a confidential messenger to her, bearing an impressive letter of credit. The odd creature rejected his offer. The Jew was in despair. The messenger said to him: 'Why get so upset? You want to sleep with a pretty woman; nothing could be easier, and you can even sleep with one prettier than this one you're pursuing. I mean my wife, whom I'll let you have for the same price.' No sooner said than done. The messenger keeps the letter of credit and the Jew sleeps with the messenger's wife. The letter of credit falls due. The Jew challenges it and denies its validity. The case comes to trial. The Jew thinks: that man will never dare admit how he came into possession of the letter, so I won't pay. At the hearing he questions the messenger . . . 'From whom did you obtain this letter of credit?' 'From you . . .' 'Is it for a loan? . . .' 'No . . .' 'Is it for goods received? . . .' 'No . . .' 'Is it for services rendered? . . .' 'No. But that's not the point. I own it. You signed it, and you'll pay it . . .' 'I did not sign it . . .' 'Are you saying I'm a forger?' 'You or someone whose agent you are . . .' 'I'm despicable, but you're a swindler. Believe me, you'd be wise not to push me too far. I'll tell the whole story. I'll be dishonoured but I'll see you ruined.' The Jew ignored the threat and the messenger revealed everything at the next hearing. They were both censured and reprimanded; the Jew was condemned to pay, and the moneys applied to the relief of the poor. It was then that I left him. I returned here. What should I do? For it was either die of starvation or do something. All kinds of projects ran through my head. At one moment I'd be planning to set off on the morrow for the provinces and attach myself to some itinerant troop of actors or musicians—whether good or bad at either, who cared? The following day I'd be thinking of having a sign painted with multiple scenes, the sort you see stuck up on a pole at a crossroads, where I'd bellow at the top of my lungs: 'See the town where he was born; see him bidding farewell to his father the apothecary, see him arriving in the capital and looking for his uncle's house; here he is on his knees before his uncle who turns him away, and here he is with a Jew, etc., etc.' The next day I'd get up determined to join some band of street singers, not the worst idea I had, for we'd have gone and serenaded under my dear uncle's windows and he'd have kicked the bucket from rage. But I chose a different path.

There he stopped, moving successively from the stance of a man holding a violin and tightening the strings as hard as he can, to that of a poor devil who's utterly exhausted, worn out, trembling at the knees, ready to drop unless someone flings him a crust of bread; he was indicating his extreme hunger by pointing at his half-open mouth; then he added: 'Need I say more? They'd toss me a chunk of bread. There'd be three or four of us there—starving—and we'd fight over it; *you* try thinking great thoughts and accomplishing great deeds, when you're that destitute.'

ME: It's hard to do.

HIM: One thing led to another, and I fetched up with them. I lived there in royal comfort. I've left. First thing I must do is crop the gut and get back to the finger-pointing-at-the-gaping-mouth business. Nothing lasts in this world. Today, you're right up at the top, tomorrow you're down at the bottom. Damned circumstance leads us, and does it very badly.

[Then, gulping down what remained in the bottle, and turning to his neighbour:] Monsieur, be so kind, just a tiny pinch of snuff? You've a handsome box there. You're not a musician? No . . . Lucky for you; the poor buggers, they're certainly to be pitied. Fate decreed that I, Rameau, should be one; whereas in Montmartre, in a windmill, there's perhaps a miller or miller's boy who'll never hear anything but the sound of the ratchet, and who might have created the loveliest melodies. Rameau, in a mill? Get yourself off to a mill, that's where you belong.

ME: Whatever a man works hard at, Nature destined him for it.

HE: She makes some peculiar blunders. For my part, I'm unable to see anything from that tremendous height where every-thing looks the same—the man with shears pruning a tree, and the caterpillar gnawing one of its leaves, so that all you see are two different insects, each doing its job. Perch yourself on Mercury's epicycle* and, like Réamur who classified flies into seamstresses, measurers, and reapers, classify humankind into joiners, carpenters, messengers, dancers, singers, you decide. I want no hand in it. I'm of *this* world and this is where I'm staying. But if it's natural to have an appetite—for I invariably come back to appetite, to the sensation I'm always conscious of—then I think it's no part of a proper system ever to be without food to eat. What a devil of an economy, some men glutted with food while others, whose stomachs are just as importunate, and whose appetite returns just as pre-dictably, can't even find a crust to chew on. The worst thing about being in want is the physical constraint it forces upon us. The destitute don't walk like other men; they leap, creep, wriggle, crawl; they spend their days adopting and performing positions.

ME: What do you mean by positions?

HIM: Go and ask Noverre. The world offers many more examples of them than his art is capable of imitating.

ME: But now you're up there as well, if I may borrow the
  expression from you or from Montaigne, *perched on the top of
  Mercury's epicycle*, and contemplating the various pantomimes
  of humankind.

HIM: No, not so, I tell you. I'm too ungainly to climb so high. I
  leave those misty heights to the cranes. I like to stay down on
  the ground; I look around me and I take up my positions, or
  I amuse myself observing the positions others take. I'm an
  excellent mime, as you're about to see.

Then he begins to smile, to mimic a man who admires, who
entreats, who defers; he stands with one foot forward, the other
back, bowed over, head up, eyes seemingly fixed upon another's
eyes, mouth half open and arms reaching towards some object;
he's awaiting an order, he receives it; off he flies like an arrow, he
returns. He's carried it out; he reports. Ever watchful, he picks
up something that falls, places a cushion or a stool beneath someone's feet, holds a saucer, pulls out a chair, opens a door, closes a
window, draws the curtains; he keeps his eye on the master and
mistress, standing motionless, arms hanging at his sides and legs
together; he's listening, trying to read faces. Then he adds: 'That
was my pantomime, it's much the same as the one flatterers,
courtiers, footmen, and beggars perform.'

Sometimes the antics of this man, like the stories of the
Abbé Galiani* and Rabelais's extravaganzas, prompt me to reflect
deeply. They're three storehouses which supply me with absurd
masks I set on the faces of the gravest personages. I see Pantaloon*
in a prelate, a satyr in a presiding judge, a pig in an ascetic monk,
an ostrich in a minister, a goose in his principal secretary. 'But by
your calculation,' I said to my companion, 'there must be a great
many beggars in this world of ours, for I know nobody who hasn't
mastered a few steps of your dance.'

HIM: You're quite right. In the entire kingdom, there's only
  one man who walks—the Sovereign. All the others take up
  positions.

ME: The Sovereign? You don't think there might even be something to say about him? You don't think that now and again he
might notice a little foot, a little coil of hair, a little nose beside
him, that would prompt him to perform a little pantomime?
Whoever needs someone else is himself needy, and assumes a
position. The King takes up a position before his mistress and
before God; he performs his steps in the pantomime. The
minister, when he's before his King, performs the steps of the
courtier, the sycophant, the footman, or the beggar. The crowd
of power-seekers take up your positions in a hundred different
ways, each baser than the last, in the presence of the minister.
As does the fashionable Abbé, dressed in his bands and long
cloak, at least once every week, in the presence of the Controller of Benefices. Upon my word, what you call the beggars'
pantomime, is what keeps the world going round. Each of us
has his little Hus and his Bertin.

HIM: I find that consoling.

But while I was speaking he kept imitating, to hilarious effect,
the positions of the personages I named; for example, he did the
little Abbé by placing his hat under his arm, his breviary in the
left hand, and holding up the train of his cloak with the right;
poking his head forward, slightly tilted towards the shoulder, and
casting his eyes down: such a consummate imitation of the hypocrite that I felt I was watching the author of *The Refutation*
petitioning the Bishop of Orléans.* He grovelled on the ground to
mimic sycophants and power-seekers—he was Bouret, before the
Auditor-General.

ME: That's quite brilliant [I told him]. However, there's one
person who's exempt from playing a part in the pantomime. I mean the philosopher, who has nothing and asks for
nothing.

HIM: And where is such a creature to be found? If he has nothing
he'll suffer; if he asks for nothing, he'll get nothing, and he'll
go on suffering.

ME: No. Diogenes scoffed at need.

HIM: But you have to be clothed.

ME: No. He went naked.

HIM: It could be cold in Athens.

ME: Less so than here.

HIM: People ate there.

ME: Undoubtedly.

HIM: At whose expense?

ME: Nature's. Where does the savage turn for food? To the earth, to animals, to fish, to trees, to plants, to roots, to streams.

HIM: A poor table.

ME: It's a generous one.

HIM: But badly served.

ME: Nevertheless it's the one we clear away, to supply our own table.

HIM: But you'll agree that our chefs, pastry-cooks, spit-turners, caterers, and confectioners add something further of their own. Considering the austere diet of your Diogenes, he can't have had a very refractory digestion.

ME: You're mistaken. The habit of the Cynic used to be the same as our monastic habit, and possessed the same virtue. The Cynics were the Carmelites and Franciscans of Athens.

HIM: Now I've got you! So Diogenes must have done the pantomime dance, if not for Pericles, at any rate for Laïs or Phryne.

ME: Once again you're mistaken. The others paid highly for the courtesan, but she gave herself to him for pleasure.

HIM: What if the courtesan was busy, and his desire urgent?

ME: He went back into his barrel, and did without.

HIM: And you're advising me to do as he did?

ME: I'd stake my life that would be better than grovelling, licking boots, and prostituting yourself.

HIM: But I need a good bed, a good table, a warm coat in winter and a cool one in summer, rest, money, and many other things for which I'd rather be indebted to benevolence than earn by toil.

ME: The fact is that you're an idle, greedy coward, with the soul of an earth-worm.

HIM: I believe I already told you that.

ME: The material things in life are certainly to be valued, but you're not taking into account the sacrifice you're making to obtain them. You are dancing, you've been dancing, and you're going to go on dancing that vile pantomime.

HIM: True. But it hasn't cost me much and now it doesn't cost me anything more. That's why it would be a mistake for me to assume a different posture that would be difficult for me, and that I wouldn't be able to maintain. But I see from what you've been telling me that my poor little wife was something of a philosopher. She was as brave as a lion. There were times when we had nothing to eat, and no money. We'd sold almost all our clothes. I'd fling myself down on the end of our bed, racking my brains to think of someone who'd lend me a few francs, which I didn't intend to repay. But she, happy as a lark, would be sitting at her harpsichord, playing and singing. She had the voice of a nightingale; I'm sorry you never heard her. When I was engaged for a concert, I'd take her with me. On the way, I'd say to her: 'Now, Madame, get yourself admired, show off your talent and your charms. Dazzle us with your *brio*, your inverted chords.' We'd arrive; she'd sing, she'd dazzle with her *brio*, her inversions. Alas, I've lost her, the poor little thing. Apart from her talent, she had a mouth as tiny as the circumference of your little finger, teeth like a row of pearls, eyes, feet, skin, cheeks, breasts, gazelle-like legs, thighs, and buttocks to inspire a sculptor. Sooner or later she'd have had the chief tax collector, at the very least. Her walk, her behind! Ah, God, what a behind!

Whereupon he began imitating his wife's walk—tiny mincing steps, nose in the air, plying his fan, swaying his behind; it was the most laughable, most ridiculous caricature of our little coquettes.

Then, picking up the thread of his discourse, he added: 'I used to take her out everywhere, to the Tuileries, to the Palais Royal, to the Boulevards. It was impossible to believe that I could keep her. If you'd seen her crossing the road in the morning, in her short jacket, bare-headed, you'd have stopped to look at her; you could have circled her waist with your thumbs and forefingers without having to squeeze. The men following her, as they watched her trot along on her tiny feet, tried to gauge the size of that ample behind whose contours were suggested by her flimsy petticoats, and would speed up their pace; she'd let them catch up with her, and then promptly turn her huge, brilliant black eyes upon them, stopping them in their tracks. For the right side of the medal did not mar the reverse. But, alas, I've lost her, and with her all my hopes of fortune. That was the only reason I'd taken her, as indeed I'd confided to her; and she was too wise not to grasp that my plan was assured of success, and too sound of judgement not to approve of it.'

Then, starting to sob and sigh, he said: 'No, no, I'll never get over it. Since it happened, I've taken to wearing clerical bands and cap.'

ME: From grief?

HIM: If you like, but actually so that I can carry my dinner-bowl on my head. But let's see what the time is, because I'm going to the Opéra.

ME: What's on?

HIM: Something of Dauvergne's. There are plenty of lovely passages in his music; it's a pity he wasn't the first to compose them. A few among the dead invariably manage to upset the living. What can we do? *Quisque suos patimur manes.** But it's half-past five; I can hear the bell ringing vespers* for Abbé Cannaye, and for me. Farewell, Monsieur Philosopher; isn't it true that I am always the same?

ME: Alas yes, unfortunately.

HIM: Here's hoping that I continue to enjoy that particular misfortune for another forty or so years. He that laughs last, laughs best.

FIRST SATIRE

Quot capitum vivunt, totidem capitum milia
(HORACE, *Satires*, II. i)*

TO MY FRIEND, MONSIEUR NAIGEON
ON A PASSAGE FROM THE
FIRST SATIRE OF HORACE'S SECOND BOOK:

Sunt quibus in Satyra videor nimis acer et ultra
*Legem tendere opus.**

FIRST SATIRE

My friend, have you not observed that reason, the prerogative peculiar to us humans, takes such a range of forms that within it alone we find parallels to every variation of instinct in animals? Consequently, there is no animal, whether benign or harmful, anywhere in the sky, the forest, or the waters of the earth, which you cannot recognize in the biped figure of man. There's the man wolf, the man tiger, the man fox, the man mole, the man hog, the man sheep—and this last is the commonest. There's the man eel—grasp him as firmly as you can, he will escape you; the man pike, who devours everything; the man snake, who twists himself into a hundred different shapes; the man bear, whom I find not unpleasing; the man eagle, soaring high in the skies above us; the man crow; the man sparrow-hawk; the man, and the bird, of prey. Nothing is rarer than a man who is wholly a man; there's not one of us without a trace of his animal counterpart.

Therefore, for every man, there's a different cry.

There's nature's cry, which I hear in what Sara says of the sacrifice of her son: *God would never have asked it of his mother.** And when Fontenelle, witness to the advance of unbelief, declared: *I'd very much like to be here sixty years from now, to see what comes of this.** Of course he wanted to be here. We do not want to die, and the end always comes a day too soon. In one more day we'd have discovered the squaring of the circle.

Why should this cry of nature, which is peculiar to us, be so rare in the imitative arts? Why is it that the poet who captures it amazes and transports us? Might it be because he thereby reveals to us the secret of our hearts?

There's the cry of passion, which I hear when Hermione asks Oreste: *Who told you so?* and when Phèdre, responding to: *They'll never meet again*, says: *They'll love one another forever.** I hear it as I depart after an eloquent sermon on almsgiving, in the mutterings of the miser at my side: *That makes one wish one were a beggar*;

93

or again, when the faithless mistress, surprised by her lover *in flagrante delicto*, reproaches him: *Ah, you no longer love me, for you'd rather believe what you've seen than what I tell you*; and yet again, in the remark of the dying usurer to the priest who exhorts him to repent: *This crucifix, I couldn't in good conscience lend more than a hundred écus on it, and then only with a note of hand.*

There was a time when I loved the theatre, particularly the opera. I was at the Opéra one evening, seated between the Abbé de Canaye, whom you know, and a certain Montbron, author of some pamphlets which are lavish with acid and sparing, very sparing, with talent. I had just listened to a poignant piece whose words and music had filled me with rapture. At that period we had never heard Pergolesi, and we thought Lully sublime. In my ecstasy I seized my neighbour Montbron by the arm and asked: 'That was beautiful, do you not agree, Monsieur?' He had a yellowed complexion, black, bushy eyebrows, and hooded, ferocious eyes; he replied: 'No, I don't feel that.' 'You don't feel that?' 'No, I am insensible to such things.' I shiver, and move away from the two-legged tiger; I go up to the Abbé de Canaye and ask him: 'Monsieur l'Abbé, what did you think of that piece they've just sung?' The Abbé answers me in accents of cold disdain: 'Good enough, I suppose, not bad.' 'And you know of something better?' 'Far, far better.' 'What is it?' 'Some lines written about that poor Abbé Pellegrin:

> His ragged breeches, string-girt, a virtual net,
> Let us behold a bum that's blacker yet.

Now that's what I call beautiful!'

How many different bird-songs, how many discordant cries just within the forest we call society! 'Come, drink this rice water.' 'What did it cost?' 'A mere nothing.' 'But how much?' 'Perhaps five or six sous.' 'What does it matter whether I die of my malady, or of theft and pillage?' 'You who are so fond of talking, how can you listen so long to that man?' 'I'm waiting; if he coughs or expectorates, he's done for.'* 'Who is that man sitting on your right?' 'He's a man of great ability who is an exceptionally good listener.' The latter says to the priest who tells him that the Lord is approaching: *I recognize him by his mount. That's how he entered into Jerusalem* ... The former, less caustic, spares himself, on his deathbed, the annoyance of being preached to by the priest who administered the last rites, by asking him: 'Monsieur, can I be of no further service to you?' There we hear the cry that reveals character.

Beware of the man monkey. He has no character, but he has many different cries.

'Doing this will bring no harm to you, but it will spell disaster for your friend.' 'Oh, what do I care, as long as it saves me?' 'But your friend . . .' 'Think of my friend as much as you wish, but of me first.' 'Do you believe, Monsieur l'Abbé, that it gives Madame Geoffrin great pleasure to receive you in her home?' 'Why should that trouble me, as long as I enjoy being there?' Watch that man when he enters a room; he lets his head drop down onto his chest, he embraces himself, he hugs himself tightly so as to be closer to himself. You've just seen the posture and heard the cry of the selfish man, a cry that echoes on all sides. It is one of nature's cries.

'It's true that I entered into this agreement with you, but I'm declaring now that I don't intend to abide by it.' 'You don't intend to abide by it, Monsieur le Comte! And why is that, may I ask?' 'Because I'm more powerful than you . . .' The cry of power is yet another of nature's cries. 'You'll think me infamous, but I don't give a damn . . .' That's the cry of shamelessness.

'But I do believe these are Toulouse goose livers?' 'Superb! Delicious!' 'Ah! Why am I not afflicted with an ailment for which these would be the remedy!' Such is the lament of a glutton who suffers from his digestion.

*In masticating them, my lord, you paid them a signal honour.** There goes the cry of the flatterer, of the despicable courtier. But there are many others.

The cries of man assume an infinite variety of forms according to the profession he follows. Frequently, they disguise the natural tone of character.

When Ferrein said: 'My friend fell sick, I treated him, he died, I dissected him;' was Ferrein a callous man? I do not know.

'Doctor, you're very late.' 'True. That poor Mademoiselle de Thé* has passed on.' 'She's dead!' 'Yes. My presence was required at the opening of the body; I don't know when anything has ever given me greater pleasure . . .' When the Doctor spoke like that, was he a callous man? I do not know. My friend, you know what enthusiasm for one's calling is like. The satisfaction of having guessed the hidden cause of Mademoiselle de Thé's death made the Doctor forget that he was speaking of his dear friend. Once his enthusiasm had evaporated, did the Doctor weep for his friend? If you ask me that, I'll admit that I don't believe he did.

Take it away, take it away, it's badly made. The man who says this about a poor-quality crucifix he's given to kiss is not ungodly. His words spring from his profession: they're the words of a dying sculptor.

That amusing Abbé de Canaye, whom I've mentioned to you, wrote a very sour, funny satire of the little *Dialogues* that his friend Rémond de Saint-Mard had composed.* One day the latter, unaware that the Abbé had written the satire, was complaining to a lady—a mutual friend—about this spiteful work. While the thin-skinned Saint-Mard continued his exaggerated moaning over a pinprick, the Abbé, who was standing behind him facing the lady, admitted his authorship and made fun of his friend by sticking out his tongue. Some declared that the Abbé's behaviour was ungentlemanly, others saw it simply as a mischievous prank. This ethical issue was tried before the court of the erudite Abbé Fénel; the only opinion anyone could ever extract from him was that sticking the tongue out had been a custom of the ancient Gauls . . . What do you conclude from that? That the Abbé de Canaye was a malicious man? That's my opinion. That the other Abbé was a fool? No, that I deny. He was a man who'd used up his eyes, and his life, on scholarly research, and who saw nothing in this world of any importance compared with the restitution of a missing passage or the discovery of an ancient custom. It's the counterpart of the geometer who, tired of the praises with which all Paris rang when Racine gave his *Iphigénie*, decided to read this highly acclaimed *Iphigénie*. He picks up the play and retires to a corner; he reads a scene, then a second; at the third he tosses the book away, saying: 'What does that prove?' It's the judgement and the language of a man accustomed from his early youth to write at the bottom of every page: *QED*.

You make yourself ridiculous, but you're neither ignorant nor silly, even less are you bad, for seeing nothing beyond your own concerns.

Imagine me tormented by regular attacks of vomiting; I spew forth gallons of a caustic, clear liquid. I'm frightened, and send for Thierry. The Doctor smiles as he examines the fluid that has issued from my mouth and fills an entire bowl . . . 'Well, Doctor, what's wrong with me?' 'You're a most fortunate man; you've restored to us the vitreous phlegm of the Ancients, which we'd lost . . .' I smile in my turn, and think no better, and no worse, of Doctor Thierry.

There are so many, many cries intrinsic to a man's occupation, that even someone more patient than you would be utterly exhausted, were I to tell you of all those that come to mind as I write. When a monarch, who personally commands his forces, says to his officers after they abandon an attack in which they would all have perished uselessly: *What were you born for, if not to die?* . . . he is uttering a cry of his profession.

When some grenadiers beg their general to show mercy to one of their brave comrades who's been caught plundering, and say: *General, give him to us. You would put him to death; we know a more severe punishment for a grenadier: he shall not take part in the first battle you win* . . ., they speak with the eloquence of their profession, a sublime eloquence! Woe betide the man with the heart of bronze who is not swayed by it! Tell me, my friend, would you have had him hanged, that soldier who was so well defended by his comrades? No. Nor would I.

Sire, that cannonball! . . . *What's that cannonball to do with the dispatch I'm dictating?* . . . *It's blasted my mess bowl to bits, but it hadn't any rice in it*. The question was asked by a king,* the

97

response uttered by a soldier, but they were both brave men; neither was a creature of the state.

Were you present when the castrato Caffarelli filled us with a rapture greater than anything that your fervour, Demosthenes, or your melodious cadences, Cicero, or your lofty genius, Corneille, or your tenderness, Racine, ever inspired in us? No, my friend, you were not present. What a lot of time we've wasted, what a lot of pleasure we've missed through not knowing one another! Caffarelli sang, and we were dazed with admiration. I turned to the famous naturalist Daubenton with whom I was sharing a sofa. 'Well, Doctor, what do you think of him?' 'His legs are frail, his knees rounded, his thighs heavy, his hips broad; possibly a being deprived of the organs that characterize his sex tends to mimic the bodily structure of the opposite sex . . .' 'But that heavenly music! . . .' 'Not a single hair on his chin!' 'That exquisite taste, that pathos-filled sense of the sublime, that voice!' 'It's a woman's voice.' 'It's the most beautiful, balanced, supple, true, soul-stirring voice . . .' While the *virtuoso* was making us weep, d'Aubenton was studying him with a naturalist's eye.

The man wholly dedicated to his calling, if he has genius, becomes a prodigy; if he has no genius, then unwavering application raises him above the common level of mediocrity. Happy the society in which every man keeps himself occupied with his own calling and with that alone! He whose glance attempts to encompass everything sees nothing, or sees imperfectly; he interrupts constantly, and contradicts the man who is speaking, and who has observed accurately.

I can hear you from here, you're saying to yourself: God be praised! I'd had quite enough of those cries of nature, of passion, of character, of profession: finally I've heard the last of them . . . You're wrong, my friend. After citing so many impolite or idiotic remarks, I'm asking your patience for one or two that are different. 'Chevalier, how old are you?' 'Thirty.' 'I'm twenty-five; well, you'd love me for sixty years or so, it's not worth beginning, for so short a time . . .' 'That must be a prude speaking.' 'And your response is that of a man with no principles, it's the reaction of joy, of wit, and of virtue. Each sex has its own language; the man's has neither the lightness, nor the delicacy, nor the sensitivity of the woman's. The one seems always to command and to affront, the other to complain and to entreat . . . And now for the words of the celebrated Muret, and then I'll move on to other topics.

Muret falls ill while travelling, and is taken to hospital. He's placed in a bed beside the litter of an unfortunate victim of one of those maladies that mystify practitioners of the healing arts. The doctors and surgeons confer about his condition. One of the consultants suggests an operation that is equally as likely to kill as to cure the patient. Opinions are divided. They are inclining towards letting Nature determine the fate of the sick man, when one of them, bolder than his colleagues, says: *Faciamus experimentum in anima vili.* That is the cry of the wild animal. But from within the curtains which surround Muret comes the cry of the man, the philosopher, the Christian: *Tanquam foret anima vilis, illa pro qua Christus non dedignatus est mori . . .** Muret's words prevented the operation, and the patient recovered.

To this medley of the cries of nature, of passion, of character, of profession, add the distinctive timbre of the national character, and you will hear the aged Horace say of his son: *That he should die,** and the Spartans say of Alexander: *Since he wishes to be God, let him be God.** These words do not reveal the character of a single man, but the general character of a nation.

I shall say nothing of the mind and manners of the clergy, nobility, and magistrature. Each has its own style of commanding, entreating, and complaining. This style is traditional. Individual members can be base or grovelling, but the class as a whole preserves its dignity. The remonstrances of our historical assemblies, however, have not always been masterpieces, although Thomas, that most eloquent man of letters, that loftiest, most admirable of souls, would not have signed his name to them; he would not have settled for something inferior, he would have gone beyond.

All this is why, my dear friend, I shall never be in a hurry to enquire about a newcomer to a social group. Such a question is often impolite, and almost always useless. With a little patience, you avoid troubling either the master or the mistress of the house, and you allow yourself the pleasure of guessing.

These precepts did not originate with me, but were given me by a very astute man* who demonstrated their application, in my presence, at Mademoiselle D***'s,* the night before I set off on that immense journey which I undertook in spite of your objections.* During the course of the evening a gentleman arrived whom my friend did not know; this person spoke quietly, carried himself easily, expressed himself elegantly, and behaved with chilly politeness. 'This man,' he whispered in my ear, 'is someone attached to the Court . . .' Then he observed that, almost invariably, he kept his right hand upon his chest, fingers together and nails facing out . . . 'Aha!' he added, 'he's an exempted officer of the Lifeguards, all that's missing is his baton.' Shortly afterwards, the man in question told a little story. 'There were four of us,' he said, 'Madame and Monsieur Such-and-such, Madame de ***, and myself.' Whereupon my instructor continued: 'Now I have the full picture. My man's married, the woman whom he mentioned third is surely his wife, and he's given me his own name in naming her.'

We left Mademoiselle D***'s house together. It was not yet too late to take a walk; he suggested a stroll round the Tuileries and I agreed. As we walked, he made many subtle, penetrating observations, expressing himself in language that was equally so; but as I'm a very plain, straightforward man, and the subtlety of his remarks obscured their true meaning for me, I begged him to clarify them with a few examples. Limited minds require examples. He was kind enough to comply, and said:

'I was dining one day as a guest of the Archbishop of Paris. I know few of the people who frequent the Archbishop, a fact which troubles me little; however, one's neighbour, the person seated beside one at table, is quite another matter. One has to know with whom one is conversing, and to succeed in this one only has to let him talk, and then piece the evidence together. I had someone on my right to decipher. In the first place, the Archbishop spoke to him only rarely, and then rather curtly;

either he's not devout, I thought, or else he's a Jansenist . . . A passing remark about the Jesuits told me that the latter was the case. A loan was being negotiated for the clergy, and I used the opportunity to question my man about the resources of the church. He gave me a full and detailed account of them, complained that the church was overtaxed, lashed out against the Minister of Finance, and added that he'd had it out in no uncertain terms in 1750 with the Comptroller of Taxes. I then realized that he'd been Agent to the clergy. In the course of the conversation he led me to understand that, had he wished it, he could have become a bishop; I supposed he must be well-born. However, as he boasted, more than once, of an elderly uncle who was a Lieutenant-General, but didn't breathe a word about his father, I deduced that he was a *parvenu* who'd made a blunder. He recounted scandalous stories involving a number of bishops, a clear indication that he possessed a malicious tongue. He went on to tell me that, in spite of intense competition, he's succeeded in getting his brother named as Administrator of ***. You'll agree that, had I been informed, on taking my seat at the table, that he was a Jansenist, humbly born, arrogant and scheming, that he hated his colleagues and that they hated him, in short that he was the Abbé of ***, I wouldn't have learnt anything more than what I discovered, and I'd have been deprived of the pleasure of discovery.'

The crowds on the Grande Allée* were beginning to lessen. My companion pulled out his watch and said to me: 'It's getting late, I'll have to leave you, unless you'd care to join me for supper.— Where?—Near here, at Mademoiselle Arnoud's.—I'm not acquainted with her.—Must one be acquainted with a courtesan to go to her house for supper? In any case, she's a charming creature, who's quite at home both with her own kind and with people of fashion. Do come, you'll enjoy yourself.—Thank you, but no; however, I'm going in that direction, so I'll keep you company as far as the cul-de-sac Dauphin . . .—We set off, and on the way he repeated to me some of Arnoud's cynical witticisms, and some of her artless, sensitive remarks. He told me of

all the regulars he met there, adding a comment about each one
. . . Applying to this same man the principles that he had given
me, I saw that he frequented both high society and low company.—Doesn't he write verse, you ask?—Very good verse.—
Wasn't he a friend of Field-Marshal de Richelieu?*—A close
friend.—Isn't he paying his addresses to the Countess
d'Egmont?—Assiduously.—Isn't there some story or other about
him? . . .—Yes, something that happened in Bordeaux, but I
don't believe it. People here are so spiteful, they circulate so many
stories, there are so many rogues who want to bring everyone
down to their own level!—Has he read you his *Russian Revolution*?*—Yes.—What do you think of it?—I think it's a historical
novel that's quite well written and very interesting, a blend of lies
and truths that our descendants will liken to a chapter of Tacitus.

And now you'll tell me that instead of having elucidated a
passage from Horace, I've very nearly given you a satire in the
style of Persius.*—That's right.—And you think I'm going to let
you off with that?—No.

You know Burigny?—Who doesn't know that honourable and
learned old man, who is Madame Geoffrin's faithful disciple?
He's very good, and very learned.—A bit odd.—Yes, I agree.—
Highly inept.—And all the better for it. One should always
provide a little absurdity for the entertainment of one's friends
. . . So? What of Burigny?—I was chatting to him, I don't recall
about what. In the course of our exchange I chanced to touch on
his favourite topic, erudition, whereupon my learned friend
interrupted me, and launched into a digression that just went on
and on.—He does that all the time, and never without one learning something as a result.—And I learned that a passage of
Horace that I'd thought rather gloomy and dull, was full of natural charm and exquisite subtlety.—Which passage?—The one
where the poet maintains that he won't be denied an indulgence
that was certainly accorded to his compatriot Lucilius.* Whether
Lucilius was Apulian or Lucanian, says Horace,* I'll follow in his
footsteps.—I understand, and it's into the mouth of Trebatius,
whose favourite text Horace has mentioned, that you put the long

discussion on the early history of both countries. That was very good, very perceptive.—How credible do you find it, the poet knowing all those facts? And even if he knew them, that he should be so lacking in taste as to abandon his topic and launch into the tedious minutiae of ancient history!—My thoughts exactly.— Horace says: *Sequor hunc, Lucanus an Apulus.* The learned Trebatius takes both sides, and says to Horace: 'Let's be entirely clear. You're neither from Apulia nor Lucano, you're from Venosa, and you labour in both vineyards. You've replaced the Sabellians, after they were expelled. Your ancestors were put there as a barrier to halt the incursions of the Lucanians and the Apulians. They filled that vacuum, and kept our territory safe against two violent enemies. At least, that's according to a very old tradition.'—The learned Trebatius, ever learned, instructs Horace in the outdated chronicles of his country. The learned Burigny, ever learned, elucidates a difficult passage in Horace for me, by interrupting me exactly in the way the poet was interrupted by Trebatius.—And you yourself use that as an excuse to treat me to a lengthy disquisition about cries of nature and expressions of passion, character and profession?—Quite true. Horace's addiction is writing verse, Trebatius's and Burigny's is discussing ancient history, mine is moralizing, and yours . . .—You don't have to tell me, I know what mine is.—Then I'll say no more. My best to you, and to all our friends of the Rue Royale* and the Cour de Marsan;* keep me in your thoughts, as I do you in mine.

Post-scriptum. I'd love to read the commentary on Horace by Abbé Galiani, if you own it.* Some time when you have a free moment I wish you'd read the third Ode of Book III, *Justum et tenacem propositi virum*,* and then explain to me the role of the verse: *Aurum irrepertum et sic melius situm*,* which has nothing to do with what precedes it, or with what follows it, and spoils everything.

As to the two lines of the tenth Epistle in Book I, *Imperat aut [servit] collecta pecunia cuique, Tortum digna sequi, potius quam ducere funem*,* this is how I interpret them:

The outlying areas of towns are frequented by poets seeking
solitude, and by rope-makers who find plenty of room there for
making rope. *Collecta pecunia*, that's the tow they collect in their
apron. The tow is, in turn, controlled by the rope-maker, and
then is itself in control of the action of the *chariot*. It's controlled
when it's being spun, it's in control when it's being twisted. For
the second operation, one end of the spun cord is attached to the
swivel hook on the spinning wheel, and the other to the swivel
hook on the *chariot*, an object rather like a small sled. This sled
carries a heavy weight to slow it down as it moves in the opposite
direction to the rope-maker, who, as he spins, walks backwards
away from the spinning wheel. Meanwhile the *chariot*, as it twists,
moves towards the spinning wheel. As the spun cord is twisted by
the action of the spinning wheel it grows shorter, and in so doing
pulls the sled towards the wheel. In this manner Horace makes us
see that money, like tow, must do the work of the *chariot* and not
of the rope-maker, must follow the twisted rope and not spin it,
must render our life more stable, more vigorous, but not control
it. The choice and placing of the words that the poet employs
indicate that, metaphorically, he was borrowing from a process he
had actually watched, and rescued from the pedestrian by his
exquisite taste.

APPENDIX

GOETHE ON *RAMEAU'S NEPHEW*

BY CHRISTOPHER WELLS

GOETHE is not merely the first translator of *Rameau's Nephew*, he is one of the work's first readers, and its first critic. The following selection is taken from his extensive writings about the work.

The full edited text of Goethe's translation together with all his writings on the text and extensive commentary may be found in Johann Wolfgang Goethe, *Sämtliche Werke*, Volume 11, *Benvenuto Cellini, Übersetzungen I*, ed. H.-G. Dewitz and W. Pross (Frankfurt am Main: Deutscher Klassiker Verlag, 1998). All page references below are to this edition. Goethe's translation is broadly accurate, though he tones down some idioms and phrases to produce a more classically restrained effect; for example, he omits entirely the scabrous anecdote of the man nearly suffocated by his mistress's enthusiastic love-making. For a detailed list of Goethe's alterations to the text, see pp. 1320–5.

Goethe's extensive notes to the text appear following the translation itself. While these are meant to explicate references perhaps unfamiliar to his contemporary audience, Goethe also uses them to interpret his text, and the following excerpts give some examples of this. Goethe sees the intricately constructed dialogue as a masterpiece in which morality and talent are contrasted; both proponents, the philosopher 'Me' and the parasitical musician 'Him', emerge as characters whose attitudes are at odds with the ideas they express. The ruthless candour of the nephew unmasks his own hypocrisy, but also that of the philosopher whose lofty moral detachment is undermined from the outset by the erotic metaphor of his thoughts as little tarts. Goethe, taking the text as, among other things, a satire on Diderot's rival Palissot, argues that it is not legitimate to judge talent that is innate by the standards of morality: talent belongs on the wider stage of society, functions at a universal level, and, he seems to be saying, transcends the individual. The yardsticks for measuring it are acquired through application and study. On the other hand, every individual is born with a conscience and his actions are to be judged only by his immediate entourage—his wife and family, his neighbours and the authorities where he lives, that is, people who know him intimately. Since Goethe also contrasts his more provincial and 'homely' Germans in their fragmented and decentralized states with the more sophisticated French whose great (and at the time oppressive) state is represented by Parisian high society, we might also detect in this overtones of Weimar and echoes of censure directed at Goethe's own private life. But the separation of morality and art which Goethe places at the centre of his observations also shows Diderot in a partisan position against Palissot, whereas Goethe, in his note on the latter, regards him as mediocre but worthy, striving for higher things without managing always to leave the banal behind, but essentially a man to be counted among the better minds of his day. It serves Goethe's purpose, of course, not to diminish Palissot's achievements on moral grounds, since he is arguing against the legitimacy of doing so. However, it is music which lends structure and dignity to this text, in Goethe's view, and consequently his observations on French music and taste may be helpful in understanding his contemporary appreciation of *Rameau's Nephew*.

The observations on taste form the starting point for a compressed discussion of appropriateness and an argument in favour of difference in nations, societies, and individuals: *Rameau's Nephew* provides the stimulus, but not the substance, of Goethe's 'note'. On several occasions Goethe embarks on the distinction between the free man of genius and the limiting, 'mediocre' conventions required by society, and in the process he sketches cultural and intellectual differences between French and German literary audiences, and hints at the links between literatures, of which the transmission of Diderot's dialogue is an interesting and not everyday example. At one point Goethe states that the French Revolution has so changed France and French society that his notes are all the more necessary in order to help his German audience appreciate French literary and intellectual life in the pre-Revolutionary 1760s. Goethe himself, on the other hand, had had early acquaintance with French literature and had followed avidly the progressive appearance of some of the major works, since excerpts from them had been sent to reading circles in Gotha during his childhood. He was *au fait* with the major players and consequently able to savour the dialogue. Goethe is keen to compare French with German culture. As part of the attempts in the eighteenth and nineteenth centuries to

create a German national identity, it was useful to identify a recognizable centralist, French model, as opposed to the fragmented absolutist
states. This was something which Wilhelm von Humboldt admired in
the work; he wrote to Goethe on 12 April 1806: '*Rameau's Nephew*
provides the occasion, and for the Nation the material, for many
interesting observations on national differences' (see pp. 1370–1).

I. *From Goethe's* Diary (Tag- und Jahres-Hefte) *for 1804 (published 1816 / 1822)*

1804: A French manuscript, Diderot's *Nephew*, was put into my hands
by Schiller with the wish that I might translate the same. I had always
been quite particularly taken with Diderot, not, indeed, for his attitudes and way of thinking, but for his mode of writing as an author,
and I found the slim notebook lying in front of me to be of the most
exciting excellence. I had scarcely encountered anything more
impertinent and more controlled, wittier and bolder, more moral in an
immoral fashion; so I decided to undertake the translation with the
utmost willingness, whereupon I summoned forth the treasures of
literature I had read before, for the sake of my own and other people's
better understanding, and so there came into being what I appended to
the work in the form of notes, and finally I published it with Göschen.
The German translation was meant to appear first, and the original
was to be printed shortly afterwards. Convinced that this would
happen, I neglected to take a copy of the original, from which, as will
be narrated later, some very odd circumstances arose [see Section III
below]. (p. 1341)

II. *Extracts from 'Notes on Persons and Matters That Are Mentioned in the Dialogue* Rameau's Nephew' *(1805)*

Preamble

The translator had set himself the task of shedding more light on
the persons and matters mentioned and discussed in the present
dialogue and on their situations and relationships by setting down
these alphabetically arranged notes for the convenience of the reader.
Many hindrances set themselves in the way of this undertaking which

could only partially be carried out. Nevertheless, since even through this his aim could still be achieved, to some extent, it seemed expedient not to hold back what has been done at present in the expectation of a more extensive treatment at some future date. (p. 755)

Rameau's Nephew

The major text which we are presenting to the German public under this title must in all probability be counted among the most accomplished of all Diderot's works. His nation, even his friends indeed, reproached him for being able to pen excellent pages readily enough, while not being capable of producing an excellent work as a whole. Such bons mots get repeated and propagate themselves, and the reputation of an excellent individual is reduced through this without any further questioning. Those people who make this sort of judgement had probably not read *Jacques the Fatalist*; and the present text also bears witness to Diderot's felicitous capacity to combine the most disparate elements of reality into a conceptual whole. Incidentally, whatever people might think of him as a writer, both his friends and his enemies were in complete agreement that in spoken conversation nobody outdid him in vivacity, power, wit, ingenuity, and elegance.

So, by choosing a dialogue form for the present text, he was putting himself at his natural advantage, and in the process he produced a masterpiece that one admires more and more, the more one becomes familiar with it. Its rhetorical and moral purpose is complex. First, he deploys all his intellectual powers to portray flatterers and spongers in the full extent of their vileness, and in the process he does not let their patrons off lightly either. At the same time, the author is at pains to lump together all his literary enemies as just such a pack of hypocrites and toadies, and furthermore he takes the opportunity of saying exactly what he thinks and feels about French music.

However heterogeneous this last ingredient—music—may appear in the context of the others, it is notwithstanding the element that lends structure and dignity to the whole: for, while a decidedly independent character manifests itself in the person of Rameau's nephew, one capable of any baseness at the merest prompting of some external stimulus, and hence one arousing our contempt, and even hatred, these feelings are nevertheless considerably mitigated by the man's revealing himself as an imaginative and resourceful musician

not entirely devoid of talent. Also, this innate talent of the main prot-
agonist lends a considerable advantage in respect of the poetic composition itself, since the person portrayed as the representative of all
flatterers and sycophants, of a whole category, now lives and acts as an
individual, as a separately drawn being, a Rameau, as a nephew of the
great Rameau.

How splendidly these threads essential to the design from the outset
have been interwoven, what delightful diversity of entertainment
springs from the fabric of this text, how the whole work, despite the
banality of confronting a rascal and an honest man, seems to be composed of real Parisian details we leave to the discerning reader and
rereader to discover for himself. For the work has been as successfully
thought out and thought through as it is in its very conception. Yes,
even its extreme heights of frivolity, where we were not at liberty to
follow, it attains with a calculated intentionality. May it please the
owner of the French original to share it with the public with the
utmost speed; so that this classic by a dead, major literary figure may
then appear in its entirety in complete and untouched form.

An investigation of when the work was most probably written might
not be out of place at this point. Palissot's comedy *The Philosophers* is
spoken of as having just appeared, or being in the process of appear-
ing. This play was staged for the first time on 2 May 1760 in Paris. The
effect of such a public, personal satire will have been great enough on
friends and enemies alike in that most lively city.

In Germany, too, we have cases where ill-disposed individuals,
partly through pamphlets and partly from the stage, set out to do
damage to other people. But anyone who is not stung by the anguish of
the moment only needs to stay calm for a while, and in a short time
everything is back on its old course, as though nothing had happened.
In Germany only presumptuousness and false achievement have anything to fear from personal satirical attack. Everything genuine, however much attacked it may be, remains as a rule dear to the nation, and
after the clouds of dust have passed over the steady man is still visible,
proceeding on his way as before.

So the German need only increase his merit through serious application and honesty for him to be appreciated by his nation, sooner or
later; and he can afford to wait for this to happen with all the more
equanimity, given that, with the present uncoordinated state of our
fatherland each man can live and work away undisturbed in his town,

in his neighbourhood, in his house, in his own room, and that, incidentally, however much storms may rage outside and elsewhere. However, in France things were quite different. The Frenchman is a sociable animal, he lives and acts, stands and falls, in the company of his fellows. How could a French high society in Paris which so many had joined, which exercised such important influence, how could a society like that permit several of its members, indeed society itself, to be so scandalously exhibited, made ludicrous, dubious, and contemptible in the very place of its living and being? A violent reaction on its part was only to be expected.

The public, taken as a whole, is not capable of judging talent: for the axioms by which that happens are not born in us, nor does chance transfer them, but only by practice and study can we attain them; on the other hand, judging moral actions is something for which each and every individual is given the most complete yardstick by his own conscience, and everyone finds it agreeable to apply this, not to himself, but to someone else. This is why you find men of letters in particular who are keen to discredit their opponents reproaching them in public with moral weaknesses, with transgressions, imputed bad intentions and probable dire consequences of their each and every action. The real viewpoint for assessing some talented individual's achievement, poetic or otherwise, is being displaced, and they drag this man, whose special gifts are to the advantage of the world and the people in it, before the general judgement-seat of morality, in front of which in actual fact only his wife and children, his servants, and at best his fellow citizens and local authorities might have been entitled to summons him. No one belongs to the world as a moral individual. Let everyone make these fine general demands of himself and let him make good whatever is deficient with God and his own heart and let him convince his fellow man of whatever is true and good in his nature. On the other hand, as that to which Nature has particularly shaped him, as a man of power, energy, wit, and talent he belongs to the world. Everything excellent can only work for an infinite circle, so let the world accept that with gratitude and let it not imagine that it possesses the competence to sit in judgement on someone in any other respect.

Meanwhile, there's no denying that nobody gladly rejects the laudable desire to find allied to great merits of the mind and body equally great merits of the soul and heart; and this universal desire, however rarely fulfilled it is, is clear proof of the ceaseless striving for an indivisible whole which is innate in human nature as its finest heritage.

Be this as it may, in returning to our French antagonists we find that, if Palissot neglected no means of detracting from his opponents in a moral sense, Diderot in the present text makes use of everything that genius and hatred, art and bitterness have to offer to represent his opponent as the most depraved of mortals.

The intensity with which this happens would seem to suggest that the dialogue was penned in the first heat of passion, not long after the appearance of the comedy *The Philosophers*, all the more so, since in it Rameau the elder, who died in 1764, is still being mentioned as a living, active figure. Chiming with this is the fact that *Le Faux Généreux* of Le Bret, of which mention is made as a flop, came out in 1758.

Lampoons like the one we are dealing with here may have appeared quite regularly at this time, as emerges from the Abbé Morellet's *Vision de Charles Palissot* and others. They have not all been printed, and indeed the major work of Diderot remained in obscurity for a long time.

We are far from considering Palissot to be the rascal he is made out to be in the dialogue. He maintained his position as a quite upstanding individual, even through the period of the Revolution, is probably still alive, and he himself jokes in his critical writings—which betray a good brain trained over a long series of years—at the outrageous caricature of himself that his adversaries have been at pains to erect. (pp. 787–92)

Taste

'Taste, he says, taste is a thing. By God I don't know what kind of a thing he made taste into, he didn't know it himself, either.' In this passage Diderot intends to portray as ludicrous his fellow countrymen who are always uttering the word taste, with and without understanding it, and who dismiss many an important production out of hand by accusing it of lack of taste.

At the end of the seventeenth century French people did not yet use the word 'taste' on its own, but rather they lent it a particular interpretation by some adjective. They said bad or good taste, and understood only too well what they meant by it. However, you can already find in a collection of anecdotes and sayings of the time the daring proposition: 'French writers possess everything, with the single exception of taste.' If one looks at French literature from its beginnings, it emerges that genius has been making major contributions to it from very early on. Marot was a man of high calibre, and who can fail to recognize the great worth of Montaigne and Rabelais?

The man of genius, like the man with a really good mind, seeks always to expand the limits of his field to infinity. They take over into their creative ambit the most multifarious elements, and are often successful enough to have them completely under control and to be able to use them creatively. However, if such an undertaking does not succeed entirely, if the intellect is not utterly compelled to surrender to it, but if the creative endeavours attain only such a level where the intelligence can still have the advantage of them, then at once there starts up a praising and blaming by individuals, and people are convinced that perfect works can be guaranteed if we analyse punctiliously the individual elements out of which they are supposed to consist.

The French have a poet, Du Bartas, whom they no longer mention, or if they do, then only with contempt. He lived from 1544 to 1590, was a soldier and a man of the world, and he wrote countless alexandrines. We Germans, viewing as we do the circumstances of that other nation from a different perspective, feel prompted to smile when we find in his works, whose title praises him as the prince of French poets, all the elements of French poetics in one place, admittedly in an odd mixture. He tackled important, significant, and broad themes, for example, the Seven Days of Creation, where he took the opportunity of displaying in expository, narrative, descriptive, and didactic mode both his naive view of the world and the manifold knowledge he had gained in an active life. Consequently, these poems conceived in deadly earnest resemble from beginning to end affable parodies, so that they are utterly detestable to any Frenchman viewing them from the current heights of his supposedly superior culture—it would be unthinkable for a French author to bear on his scutcheon—as the Elector of Mainz does the wheel—some kind of symbolic representation of Du Bartas's *Seven Days' Labours*.

But in order to avoid getting diffuse and hence paradoxical in this aphoristic treatment of our essay, let us ask if the first forty lines of Du

Bartas's 'Seventh Day of Creation' are not after all excellent, whether they do not deserve their place in every collection of models of French writing, whether they do after all not bear comparison with many a reputable modern product? German cognoscenti will concur with us and will thank us for the attention we have drawn to this work. The French, however, will probably carry on failing to recognize all that is good and excellent in it on account of the oddities it contains.

For that constantly aspiring culture of the mind that finally came to fruition in the age of Louis XIV has at all times been at pains to distinguish precisely all poetic and spoken styles, and moreover, not by starting with the form but from the material, so that people banished certain ideas, thoughts, modes of expression, and words from tragedy, comedy, and the ode—in the case of the latter this was the very reason why they could never come to terms with it—and in their place others were adopted and prescribed in each of these spheres as especially appropriate.

They treated the different poetic genres like different societies in which a special form of behaviour is considered polite. Men, when alone amongst themselves, behave differently, and differently again when they are together with ladies, and the same company will behave differently again when joined by some person of superior social standing to whom they have reason to show deference. The Frenchman, moreover, is not reticent about speaking, even in judgements about products of the mind, of *convenances* (conventions), a word which can actually be applied only to social proprieties. One ought not to argue the rights and wrongs of the case with him, but should try to see to what extent he is right. One can but be pleased that such a witty and worldly wise nation felt constrained to try this experimentation, and is still compulsively continuing with it.

However, in the higher sense everything depends on what sphere the individual of genius has demarcated for himself in which he intends to create, and which elements he has selected to use as his material. In this he is determined partly through his own inner urgings and his own conviction and partly also by which nation and which century he is working for. In this, it must be admitted, it is the genius alone who hits the mark as soon as he brings forth works that do him credit, delighting and furthering the understanding of his contemporaries. For by wanting to compress his wider ambience into the focus of his nation, he knows how to make use of all the internal and external advantages and simultaneously to satisfy, indeed to satiate, the pleasure-seeking masses. Think of Shakespeare and of Calderón! They stand unimpeached before the highest seat of aesthetic judgement, and if some subtle analyst should stubbornly prosecute them on account of particular passages, then, with a smile, they would produce an image of that nation, of that time for which they had worked, and because of that they would not just have allowances made for them, but because they were able to adapt so successfully they would win new laurels.

The drawing of distinctions among poetic genres and styles of language lies in the nature of poetics and rhetoric themselves; but only the artist can undertake the analysis that he does in fact undertake, for he is mostly successful enough to have a feel for what belongs in this or that circle. Taste is innate in genius, even if it does not achieve perfect development in every case. From this it would admittedly be desirable that the nation might have taste in order to avoid each individual taste having to develop after its own fashion. But unfortunately the taste of those who are by nature unproductive is negative, constricting, exclusive, and in the end it saps the energy and life of the class of those who are creative.

It may well be that among the Greeks and in many Romans we find a very tasteful distinction and sublimation of the different poetic genres, but we northern peoples cannot be directed exclusively to those models. We have other ancestors to boast of, and have many other patterns in mind. If it were not the case that the romantic turn taken by uncultivated centuries had brought the monstrous into contact with the tasteless, from where would we have a *Hamlet*, a *Lear*, an *Adoration of the Cross*, a *Constant Prince* [*La devoción de la Cruz* and *El príncipe constante* by Calderón]?

Since we shall in all probability never succeed in reaching the merits of antiquity, it is our duty to have the courage to keep ourselves at the high level of these barbaric advantages, and moreover, at the same time it is our duty to make ourselves thoroughly familiar with, and to assess faithfully, what other people think, judge, and believe, and what they produce and achieve. (pp. 763–6)

Music

. . . Since everything we have just stated in general and cursory terms about the nature of music can only have the purpose of casting some light on the present dialogue, we are bound to observe that it is not without difficulty that Diderot's own standpoint permits itself to be understood.

Over half the previous century all the arts in France were mannered and set apart from all actual artistic truth and simplicity in a way that, for us, is alien and indeed almost beyond belief. Not only had the unreliable edifice of opera become ever more rigid and stiff through tradition, but tragedy itself was played out in hooped skirts, and a hollow, affected style of declamation recited its masterpieces. This went so far that that exceptional man Voltaire used to fall into an expressionless, monotonous, and, as it were, psalmonizing bombast when reading out his own plays, that actually deserved a much better treatment, and he remained entirely convinced that in doing this he was only giving proper expression to their dignity.

It was exactly the same with painting. A certain traditional kind of grotesqueness had come into vogue, to such an extent that it seemed most intrusive and intolerable to the leading intellects of the age that were developing from their own inner natural powers.

Consequently they hit collectively upon the idea of opposing what they called Nature to Culture and Art. How Diderot was in error on this issue we have expounded elsewhere, with all due respect and affection for this excellent man.

He found himself in a special situation in relation to music as well. The compositions of Lully and Rameau belong more in the category of serious than of light, popular music. What the *Bouffons* brought with them from Italy had more of the pleasing and ingratiating about it than of the serious, and yet Diderot, who is so vehemently in favour of serious music, joins himself to the latter party and looks to see his expectations satisfied by it. But it was probably rather because this new, versatile form appeared to tear down that old, hated inflexible framework, and to level a fresh surface for new efforts, which made him prize it so highly. Additionally, French composers immediately made use of the free space and commenced their old serious musical mode, but more melodically and with a greater artistic veracity, to please a new generation of listeners. (pp. 772–3)

Palissot (born in Nancy in 1730)

. . . In this play [*The Philosophers*] there appeared, namely, exaggerated poets, pretentious patrons and patronesses, bluestockings and suchlike people whose prototypes are not scarce, once Art and Science begin to make their mark in everyday life. Whatever ludicrous elements they may possess are here portrayed as exaggerated to the point of tastelessness, whereas it is always something to be thankful for when some person of note from the mass of the populace, some society beauty, a rich man, someone of rank chooses to participate in something right and good, even if they do not always set about it in the right way.

Put in absolute terms, nothing belongs less in the theatre than literature and its affairs. Everything that works and weaves in this circle is so delicate and so weighty that no contentious issue from it ought to be brought before the judgement of the gaping and gawping groundlings. And let no one cite Molière as a case, as Palissot and others after him have done. Genius is not to be prescribed to, it flits sure-footedly like a sleepwalker over the sharpest mountain ridges, from which waking mediocrity comes crashing down at the first faltering step. With what a light touch Molière treated such themes will shortly be elaborated upon elsewhere . . . (p. 774)

The Philosophers

. . . Palissot's *Philosophers* was merely an expanded version of the earlier festival play at Nancy (*Le Cercle, ou les Originaux*). He goes further, but he does not see any further. As a limited opponent of a particular situation, he has absolutely no insight into what is important at a more general level, and he produces but a cheap and momentary effect on a limited, partisan audience.

If we move to a higher plane, it does not remain hidden from us that a false semblance commonly accompanies art and learning when they go out into the real world: for they work their effects on everyone present and certainly not just on the best minds of the century. Often the part played by half-educated, pretentious natures is sterile, indeed downright harmful. Common sense is shocked at the false use of higher sentiments, especially when they are confronted directly with harsh reality.

And then again, all retiring people who devote themselves to one sole enterprise enjoy a strange respect which people readily find laughable. These individuals do not easily hide the fact that they set great store by what they spend all their lives doing, and they appear to the man who does not know how to appreciate their efforts, or to show understanding for their perhaps too keenly perceived sense of their own deserts, to be arrogant, capricious, and full of their own importance.

All of this springs from the enterprise itself, and only that individual would be praiseworthy who would appreciate how to counter such inevitable evils in such a way that the main purpose would not be missed and the higher benefits for the world of society would not be lost. But it is Palissot's intention to make a bad thing worse, he determines to write a satire to damage, in the public's opinion, certain identifiable individuals whose image at best lends itself to being distorted, and how does he set about it?

His play is concisely summed up in three acts. The economy of the work is skilful enough and attests a practised talent, only the plot is thin, one finds oneself in the all-too-familiar setting of French comedy. Nothing is new, apart from the bold step of portraying quite unambiguously recognizable individuals of the day.

Before his death an honest burgher had promised his daughter's hand to a young soldier, but the mother, presently a widow, has become enamoured of philosophy and now intends to bestow her daughter on a member of that profession. The philosophers themselves appear in a repulsive light, and yet in the main they are so unspecifically drawn that one could easily replace them with worthless wretches of any caste or class.

None of them is in any way, by affection, or habit, or anything else, bound to the lady of the house, none of them has fallen a prey to self-deception in respect of her or feels any other human emotion towards her: all that was too refined for our author, although he might have found examples enough to hand in the so-called *Bureau d'esprit*; no, his aim was to make the company of philosophers hateful. They despise and curse their patroness in the crudest fashion. These gentlemen all only set foot in the house in order to win the girl for their friend Valère. They all declare that once this plan has succeeded none of them will cross the threshold ever again. And by such traits of character we are meant to recognize men like D'Alembert and Helvétius! It is, I suppose, conceivable that the maxim of self-interest postulated by the latter may be taken to its logical conclusion and be presented as leading directly to pickpocketing. Finally some jackanapes of a servant comes in on hands and knees with a head of raw lettuce in his mouth, in order to send up the state of Nature which Rousseau portrays as desirable. An intercepted letter reveals the true attitudes of the philosophers towards the lady of the house, and they are thrown out in disgrace.

So far as its technical merit is concerned, the play was quite able to hold its own in Paris. Its versification is by no means clumsy, and here and there one finds a witty turn of phrase, but it is shot through with an appeal to everything common and vulgar, that artistic ploy of those who are the enemies of excellence, intolerable and contemptible . . . (pp. 776–8)

III. '*Notice on Diderot's* Rameau's Nephew' *(in* Über Kunst und Altertum, *iv. I, 1823)*

In the year 1805 I translated *Rameau's Nephew* by Diderot from the manuscript, which the publisher took away with him with the intention of publishing that as well once the public had taken notice of the translation. The French invasion in the following year, the passionate hatred of that people and their language which this provoked, and the long drawn-out period of misery that ensued prevented the project, which has not to this day been carried out.

However, in 1818, when it was planned to add the complete works of Diderot to the *Collection* of French prose writers and a provisional advertisement to this effect was published, this hidden manuscript was also mentioned, which was apparently known only through a German translation from which the editors gave an account of the content of this strange work in some detail, at the same time translating one or two passages back into French, not infelicitously. While not prepared to consider the work a masterpiece, they still found it worthy of the original pen of Diderot, which probably amounts to the same thing.

The matter was mentioned a few times afterwards, but without further success; finally, in 1821 there appeared in Paris *Le Neveu de Rameau dialogue, ouvrage posthume et inédit par Diderot*, and caused a great stir, as was only fitting. For a time people thought it was the original, until in the end the humorous practical joke of its being a back-translation was discovered.

To date I have not been in a position to make a comparison: but Parisian friends who were the cause of it and who accompanied the person who undertook it every step of the way assert that the work has turned out well, and would indeed have finished up better still, had the young, talented, and fiery translator stuck closer to the German.

Whether the name of this good man is already well known I could not say, nor do I consider myself at liberty to reveal his identity, although he was good enough to make himself known to me by sending me a copy as soon as the work appeared. (pp. 796–7)

EXPLANATORY NOTES

RAMEAU'S NEPHEW

1 [Epigraph] *Vertumnis . . . iniquis*: 'A man born when every single Vertumnus was out of sorts' (Horace, *Satires*, II. vii. 14; trans. H. R. Fairclough, Loeb edn.). Vertumnus was god of the changing year and could assume any shape he pleased. The reference is, in the first instance, to the mercurial personality of 'Him'; but it may also refer to 'Me'. On the relevance of this satire to the text more generally, see the Introduction.

3 *Palais-Royal*: these are the public gardens, then larger than now, situated behind the Palais-Royal. The Allée de Foy, a favourite haunt of prostitutes, was on the east side; the Allée d'Argenson was on the west side of the gardens.

Café de la Régence: this café, run by Rey from 1745, was situated in the Place du Palais-Royal. It was celebrated as a gathering-place for the best chess-players; Diderot himself used to go there to watch chess.

4 *Cours-la-Reine . . . Champs-Elysées*: the Cours-la-Reine and the Champs-Elysées were both public spaces then situated outside the city boundaries; both enjoyed dubious reputations after dark.

7 *as it pleases*: Diderot greatly admired the sixteenth-century comic writer Rabelais. His 'monk' is Frère Jean des Entommeures from *Gargantua* (1534), but this particular dictum is largely of Diderot's own invention.

11 *Mérope's soul*: heroine of Voltaire's tragedy of that name (1743); Frederick the Great thought it an 'incomparable tragedy'. Voltaire's tragedies are now unperformed and scarcely read; but for Diderot's generation they represented the peak of tragic art, surpassed only by Racine.

12 *Mahomet*: Voltaire's tragedy *Mahomet* (1742) is a strident attack on religious intolerance. Leaving nothing to chance, Voltaire dedicated the play to the pope.

Maupeou: eighteenth-century French politics is marked by a power struggle between the *parlements* (judicial bodies in Paris and the provinces, under Jansenist influence) and centralizing royal authority. Maupeou, who became chancellor in 1768, acted decisively to suppress the *parlements*. The philosophes in general, and Diderot in particular, were hostile to Maupeou's reforms, and therefore uncomprehending of Voltaire, who, against the 'liberal' tide, supported Maupeou in a series of pamphlets written in 1771.

12 *Les Indes . . . 'Nuit, éternelle nuit'*: *Les Indes galantes* is an *opéra–ballet* by Rameau. The air 'Profonds abîmes du Ténare, | Nuit, éternelle nuit' is sung by 'Envie' in the first act of Rameau's opera *Le Temple de la gloire* (the libretto is by Voltaire); the opera was performed in celebration of France's victory at the battle of Fontenoy (1745).

13 *Three Centuries . . . Heritage*: *The Three Centuries of Our Literary Heritage* (1772), by the Abbé Sabatier de Castres, is a literary history hostile to the philosophes.

15 *Soubise's coachman*: the Hôtel de Soubise had very large stables where tramps used to sleep; the building now houses the Archives Nationales (in the Rue des Francs-Bourgeois).

17 *jacket!*: see frontispiece, p. xxxvi.

18 *'Come into my cell . . .'*: a well-known anticlerical song, which begins: 'Come into my cell, | Follow me, beautiful Ursula; | With voluptuous-ness | Let us temper our austerity.'

20 *o stercus pretiosum*: 'O precious manure.'

21 *Concert spirituel*: these were regular concerts of religious music held at the château of the Tuileries (which no longer exists) from 1725. Virtuoso violinists Ludovico Ferrari and Carlo Francesco Chiabrano performed there in 1758 and 1751 respectively.

23 *Allée des Soupirs*: on the west side of the Luxembourg gardens.

24 *she's eight*: it is tempting here to identify 'Me' with Diderot, whose daughter Angélique was born in 1753. She received her first lessons in the harpsichord at the age of eight, i.e. in 1761, the approximate date of a number of the incidents referred to in this work. Angélique went on to become a highly talented harpsichordist.

27 *her little count*: the singer had a long-running affair with the Comte de Lauraguais, which was briefly broken off in late 1761. Diderot announces this news to his mistress Sophie Volland in a letter written from Paris on 2 October 1761: 'The little Comte de Lauraguais has gone off and left Mademoiselle Arnould' (*Diderot's Letters to Sophie Volland*, 96–7).

Friends of Music . . . angel: the Concerts des amateurs were a series of regular concerts, founded in 1769, and held at the Hôtel de Soubise.

Le Mercure galant: Boursault's play *Le Mercure galant* (1679) was revived in 1753, when Préville enjoyed great success, playing at least five differ-ent roles.

32 *nothing but a wit*: a reference to Mme Du Deffand's famous put-down of Montesquieu's *De l'esprit des lois* (*The Spirit of the Laws*), that it was nothing but 'de l'esprit sur les lois' ('spirit/wit about the laws').

all else is vanity: echo of Ecclesiastes 1: 2.

34 *round my neck*: compare what Diderot wrote on 2 October 1761 to Sophie
Volland: 'I can't continue to live on the incense of posterity. A delicious
meal, a touching book, a walk in a cool and solitary spot, a conversation
where you open your heart and give your emotions free rein, a strong
feeling which brings tears to your eyes, makes your heart beat faster, takes
your breath away, and plunges you into an ecstasy, whether it comes from
hearing of a generous deed or from the love you feel for someone, health,
gaiety, freedom, leisure, comfort; these are the things that make up true
happiness. I shall never be happy in any other way' (*Diderot's Letters to
Sophie Volland*, 97–8).

memory of Calas: Jean Calas, a Protestant, was unjustly put to death in
Toulouse in 1762 for the murder of his son; Voltaire mounted a public
campaign for the righting of this judicial wrong, publishing such works
as his *Traité sur la tolérance* (*Treatise on Toleration*, 1763). Calas was
finally rehabilitated in 1765, as a direct result of Voltaire's relentless
campaigning. 'Me' here contrasts *Mahomet*, the work of art attacking
religious intolerance (see note to p. 12 above), with practical action to
combat the same evil.

37 *Le Portier . . . Aretino*: the *Histoire de Dom B . . . [Bougre], portier des
Chartreux* (1741), by Gervaise de Latouche, is one of the classics of
eighteenth-century French obscene literature. The 'positions' refer to a
group of sixteen sonnets by Pietro Aretino (1492–1556) accompanying
engravings of sexual positions by the artist Giulio Romano.

39 *jaws snap shut . . .*: some details of this description recall d'Holbach,
as Diderot describes him to Sophie Volland in a letter of 1 November
1760.

45 *Ingenii largitor venter*: (Lat). 'The stomach, purveyor of genius': the
expression is from Rabelais (*Le Quart Livre*, 1552), and echoes the pro-
logue to Persius' *Satires*.

46 *Zara*: Palissot's play *Zarès* was a failure when it was first performed at the
Comédie-Française in 1751.

Le Faux généreux: Bret's play *L'Orpheline ou le Faux Généreux* (*The
Orphan, or the False Benefactor*) played for only five performances at the
Comédie-Française in January 1758. The work is exactly contemporary
with Diderot's play *Le Père de famille* (*The Father of a Family*), and the
two men felt themselves to be in competition, especially since the plots of
the two plays were somewhat similar.

47 *Les Philosophes*: Palissot's comedy *Les Philosophes* was first performed at
the Comédie-Française in May 1760; it ran for fourteen consecutive
performances, a success for the period. The play satirizes the philosophes, and Diderot in particular.

the lady theologian: reference to a play by the Jesuit Bougeant satir-
izing the Jansenists: *La Femme Docteur ou la Théologie janséniste tombée en*

quenouille (*The Lady Doctor, or Jansenist Theology Fallen into Female Hands*, 1731).

49 *L'Avare . . . Tartuffe*: Molière's comedies *L'Avare* (*The Miser*, 1668) and *Tartuffe* (1664) were in the repertoire of the Comédie-Française at this time, and already well established as classics.

50 *Opéra-Comique*: the Opéra-Comique was formed by the merger in 1759 of the Théâtre de la Foire and the Théâtre des Boulevards; in 1762 it absorbed the Comédie-Italienne.

L'Avant-Coureur . . . Le Censeur hebdomadaire: these are all journals known for being hostile to the philosophes.

51 *qui siedo . . . due coglioni*: 'I'm sitting here always like a monstrous dick between two bollocks'; it was common practice to cloak obscenity in Italian.

Messer Gaster: jokey name for the stomach, taken from Rabelais (*Quart Livre*, ch. 57).

56 *per fas et nefas*: (Lat.) 'come what may.'

dangerous scoundrels ever: the play in question is Helvétius's *L'Homme dangereux*, refused by the Comédie-Française in 1770, and finally performed in 1782.

57 *Bertinhus*: a nickname for Bertin, in which the name of his mistress is conflated with a pseudo-Latin ending *-us*.

59 *equal . . . in the sky*: Genesis 15: 4–6.

61 *san-benito . . . in readiness*: the philosophes regarded the Inquisition and its practice of the auto-da-fé, in which 'heretics' were burned at the stake, dressed in a penitent's gown or *san-benito*, as emblematic of religious intolerance. See, for example, the description of an auto-da-fé in chapter 6 of Voltaire's *Candide*.

62 *Vivat . . . imperator*: (Lat.) 'Long live Mascarille, king of the rogues'; a quotation from Molière's *L'Étourdi* (II. xi).

64 *'I'm a poor devil . . . my treasure'*: these two quotations of songs are imprecisely quoted from Duni's *L'Ile des fous* (*The Island of Fools*, 1760), scenes 4 and 9 respectively, where they are sung by the miser Sordide.

'My heart's forsaking me': aria from the opéra-comique *Maréchal-ferrant*, music by Philidor, performed at the Foire Saint-Laurent in 1761.

musices . . . source of melody: expression cited in Capella's *Artes liberales* (1658).

65 *kick in the pants*: the 'Querelle des Bouffons', a struggle between 'traditional' French music and 'new' Italian music, was triggered when the *Bouffons italiens* were invited to perform at the Opéra (1752–4). It was the performance in Paris of these works of Pergolesi which caused a sensation:

his *Stabat Mater* was performed at the *Concert spirituel* in 1753; *La Serva Padrona* (*The Servant-Mistress*) was seen in Paris in 1746 and 1752, and it was the performance of this work at the Opéra on 1 May 1753 which ignited the Querelle; his *Tracollo medico ignorante* was also given in Paris in 1753. The philosophes, in particular Diderot and Jean-Jacques Rousseau, favoured Italian music over French, as being more natural and more melodic, and more able therefore to imitate the passions; they saw French music, embodied by Rameau, as rigid, rule-bound, and inexpressive.

65 *Tancrède . . . ran forever*: these are the works typical of the 'old' French school which have been displaced by the Italians. *Tancrède* (1702) and *L'Europe galante* (1697) have music by Campra; *Issé* (1697) by Destouches; *Les Indes galantes* (*The Gallant Indies*, 1735), *Castor et Pollux* (1737) and *Les Talents lyriques ou Les Fêtes d'Hébé* (1739) are all by Rameau; *Armide* (1686) was set by Lully to a libretto by Quinault.

Rebel and Francœur: directors of the Opéra from 1757 to 1767, who had to face up to the growing rivalry of the Opéra-Comique.

back alley: the Opéra was then situated in the Palais-Royal, and was reached from the gardens by a cul-de-sac. The theatre (which had once been Molière's) burned down in 1763, and did not reopen until 1770.

Peintre . . . son modèle: *Le Peintre amoureux de son modèle* (*The Painter in Love with His Model*), an opéra-comique by Duni, his first to a French text, enjoyed an enormous success when it was first performed in 1757 at the Foire Saint-Laurent.

66 *'Go and see . . . Jean'*: the refrain of a popular song; the insinuation is 'you can bank on it'.

Ragonde and Platée: *Les Amours de Ragonde* (1742) is a comedy by Destouches, with music by Mouret. *Platée* (1745) is a burlesque *comédie-ballet* by Rameau which parodies the Italian style of singing.

their own tongue: the view that the Italian language was particularly suited to music, unlike French, was defended notably by Jean-Jacques Rousseau. Ironically, the (real) Jean-François Rameau maintained the opposite view in his *Raméide*.

67 *La Plaideuse*: *La Plaideuse* (*The Lady Litigant*, 1762), a comedy by Favart with music by Duni.

68 *I am a worthless wretch . . . si sta*: these extracts of arias (in French and Italian in the original) are taken from Duni's *L'Ile des fous* and Pergolesi's *La Serva Padrona*.

69 *'Ah, j'attendrai'*: from Roland's monologue in Lully's opera *Roland* (1685).

70 *'Pale torches . . . oblivion'*: Télaïre's aria (inaccurately cited) from Rameau's opera *Castor et Pollux* (1737). In Diderot's novel *The Nun*, Suzanne Simonin sings this aria, one of the most famous in French Baroque

opera, when she first arrives at the abbey of Longchamp (see *The Nun*, trans. R. Goulbourne, Oxford World's Classics, 24).

70 *Maximes . . . Pensées*: two of the greatest classics of the French seventeenth century, and manifestly unsuitable for musical setting.

71 *Plunge your dagger . . . reason*: this is a random mixture of extracts from Racine's tragedy *Phèdre* (1677).

72 *'Rinaldo's conqueror (if any such exists)' . . . Indes galantes*: from Armide's aria in Lully's *Armide et Renaud*, and from the chorus in the Inca act, scene 3, of Rameau's *Les Indes galantes*.

80 *boulevard*: after 1759 the 'unofficial' theatres (as opposed to the Comédie-Française and the Opéra) obtained permission to establish themselves along the busy boulevards to the north of Paris.

chimney-sweep: reference to Mme Favart playing the role of Mme Bontour in Favart's *Soirée des Boulevards* (1758).

L'Enfant . . . perdu et retrouvé: *L'Enfant d'Arlequin perdu et retrouvé* (*Harlequin's Child Lost and Found*), an adaptation from Goldoni given in Paris by the Comédie-Italienne in 1761.

Punchinello: this traditional figure from *commedia dell'arte* retained his place in the works put on every August at the Foire Saint-Laurent.

81 *Memnon's statue*: a colossal statue near Thebes (one of a pair) was damaged in an earthquake in the year 27, and thereafter it gave out a musical sound as soon as it was struck by the first rays of the sun (said to be the voice of Memnon greeting his mother, the Dawn).

Danaides: in Greek mythology the Danaides are condemned in Hades to fill a bottomless barrel. This image of prodigality seems awkward in this context.

84 *Mercury's epicycle*: the allusion is to a theory in ancient astronomy that was supposed to explain the movements of certain planets; it was made redundant by the heliocentric theory of the universe. The expression, as stated further on, is taken from Montaigne (*Essays*, i. 26 and ii. 27); it mocks an antiquated, speculative, and unempirical view of the world.

85 *Galiani*: the Abbé Galiani (see Glossary of Names) was a friend of Diderot, whom he often met at the Baron d'Holbach's. As an author, he is now remembered for his *Dialogues sur le commerce des blés* (*Dialogues on the Trade in Corn*, 1770) and for his correspondence with Mme d'Épinay. The 'stories' referred to here are recollections of verbal performances, recounted with relish by Diderot in his letters to Sophie Volland, as here, for example, on 20 October 1760: 'The Abbé tells good stories, but above all he is an excellent actor. He is quite irresistible. You would really have laughed to see him stretching out his neck and imitating the nightingale's little voice; puffing himself up and catching the cuckoo's raucous tone;

and then sticking up his ears and assuming the stupid and ponderous gravity of the donkey—all this naturally and effortlessly. He is a born mimic, every inch of him' (*Diderot's Letters to Sophie Volland*, 83).

85 *Pantaloon*: Venetian character in Italian comedy, a lean and foolish old man who is the butt of jokes; he wears spectacles and tight-fitting trousers (pantaloons).

86 *Bishop of Orléans*: the author of the *Lettres critiques ou Analyses et réfutation de divers écrits modernes sur la religion*, in 19 volumes (1753–63) is the Abbé Gabriel Gauchet; he had earlier criticized Diderot's *Pensées philosophiques*. The Bishop of Orléans referred to here, Louis Sextus de Jarente de la Bruyère, was the Controller of Benefices from 1758 to 1788.

89 *Quisque . . . manes*: 'Each endures his own particular fate' (Virgil, *Aeneid*, iv. 743). The speaker here uses *manes* to refer more particularly to 'ancestors' (i.e. Dauvergne is eclipsed by the composers who came before him and whom he imitates). The same quotation occurs in Diderot's *Salon de 1767*, also in connection with J.-F. Rameau; this is the only other reference in the whole of Diderot's work to the real-life model of Rameau's nephew.

bell ringing vespers: the Opéra rang a bell to announce the beginning of a performance, at six in the evening.

FIRST SATIRE

91 [Epigraph] *Quot capitum . . . milia*: 'For every thousand living souls, there are as many thousand tastes' (Horace, *Satires*, II. i. 27–8; trans. H. R. Fairclough, Loeb edn.).

92 [Dedication] *Sunt quibus . . . tendere opus*: 'There are some critics who think I am too savage in my satire and strain the work beyond lawful bounds' (Horace, *Satires*, II. i. 1–2; Loeb edn.). Diderot quotes again from the same poem: but this remark is aimed at his friend Naigeon.

93 *God . . . of his mother*: reference to God's asking Abraham to sacrifice his son Isaac (Genesis 22). The saying comes from Maffei's commentary on his own *Mérope*.

I'd very much . . . comes of this: this passage has not been found in Fontenelle's works; Diderot may be recording something which he heard.

Who told you so . . . forever: from two of Racine's tragedies, respectively *Andromaque* (1667) and *Phèdre* (1677).

94 '*Come, drink . . . done for.*': these exchanges are lifted almost word for word from Horace (*Satires*, II. iii. 155–7).

95 *In masticating . . . signal honour*: from La Fontaine (*Fables*, vii. 1).

96 *Mademoiselle de Thé*: the identities of this person and of the Doctor remain mysterious.

Explanatory Notes

96 *Dialogues ... had composed*: Rémond de Saint-Mard published his *Nouveaux dialogues des dieux ou Réflexions sur les passions* (*New Dialogues of the Gods, or Reflections on the Passions*) in 1711.

97 *by a king*: the king's words are quoted from Voltaire's *Histoire de Charles XII* (Book 8). The source of the soldier's reply remains unidentified.

99 *Faciamus ... est mori ...*: 'Let's try the experiment on this vile [i.e. still living] soul', to which the reply comes: 'As if it could be vile, this soul for which Christ did not disdain to die!'

That he should die: quotation from Corneille's tragedy *Horace*; Boileau had famously declared this concise reply to be a perfect example of 'sublime' discourse.

Since ... be God: from Plutarch's *Moralia*, best known in France in Amyot's translation (1572).

100 *astute man*: Naigeon explains that the man in question is Claude de Rulhière.

Mademoiselle D***'s: according to Naigeon, this refers to Mlle Dornais (or Dornet), a former dancer at the Opéra, who in the late 1760s was the mistress of Prince Galitzin. According to Diderot, in his correspondence with Sophie Volland, Naigeon had been in love with her.

that immense journey ... your objections: this refers to Diderot's trip to Russia via Holland, the one great journey of his life. He left Paris in June 1773, in the face of the objections of his friend Naigeon.

101 *the Grande Allée*: the central promenade in the Tuileries gardens.

102 *de Richelieu*: in 1758–9 Rulhière had been aide-de-camp to the Duc de Richelieu. Richelieu, grandson of the great cardinal, was a celebrated soldier and an even more celebrated libertine. The comtesse d'Egmont (1740–73) was the daughter of the Duc de Richelieu. She was the friend, and perhaps the mistress of Rulhière, who dedicated several poems to her.

Russian Revolution: Rulhière's *Histoire ou Anecdotes sur la Révolution de Russie en l'année 1762* was written at the request of the Comtesse d'Egmont. The work was eventually published in 1797, six years after Rulhière's death. Before that, Diderot had been involved in negotiations with Catherine the Great, who wanted to buy the manuscript of the work in order to prevent its publication. Rulhière had been secretary of the French Embassy at the time of Catherine's *coup d'état*, and his *Histoire* hints at her part in the death of her husband Peter III.

of Persius: the satires of Aulus Persius Flaccus (AD 34–62), influenced by Stoicism, are less gentle than Horace's. On Diderot's use of different models of satire, see Introduction.

Lucilius: a reference to Horace, *Satires*, II. i, quoted at the start of the work. Gaius Lucilius (180–103 BC) was considered the founder of Roman satire.

102 *Apulian . . . says Horace*: 'He it is I follow—I, a Lucanian or Apulian' (Horace, *Satires*, II. i. 34; trans. H. R. Fairclough, Loeb edn.).

103 *Rue Royale*: D'Holbach regularly received at his home in the Rue Royale the group of atheists he referred to as his 'synagogue'.

Cour de Marsan: Diderot's friend Mme de Maux lived in the Cour de Marsan, at the Louvre.

commentary . . . own it: Galiani wrote his commentary on Horace in French around 1764, when he was living in Paris. Extracts were published in the *Gazette littéraire de l'Europe* in 1765–6; the full commentary was published only in 1821.

Justum . . . virum: 'The man tenacious of purpose in a righteous cause . . .' (Horace, *Odes*, III. iii. 1; trans. C. E. Bennett, Loeb edn.)

Aurum . . . melius situm: 'undiscovered gold (better so bestowed, while Earth yet hides it' Horace, *Odes*, III. iii. 49; Loeb edn.).

Imperat . . . ducere funem: 'Money stored up is for each his lord or his slave, but ought to follow, not lead, the twisted rope' (Horace, *Epistles*, I. x. 47–8; trans. H. R. Fairclough, Loeb edn.).

GLOSSARY OF NAMES

Alberti Giuseppe-Mateo Alberti (1685–1751) and Domenico Alberti (1710–40), both composers of music for harpsichord.

Arnould Madeleine Sophie Arnould (1740–1802) made her debut at the Opéra in 1757, and sang in many of the operas of Rameau. She had a long-standing affair (and three children) with the Comte de Lauraguais; their affair was briefly broken off in late 1761.

Baculard François Thomas de Baculard d'Arnaud (1718–1805), a friend of Diderot in their youth, later became a collaborator of Fréron in *L'Année littéraire* from 1754; as an author, he is mainly remembered for his highly sentimental short stories.

Bagge Charles-Ernest, Baron de Bagge, a wealthy Dutch music-lover who gave at his hôtel a concert every Friday. (Diderot writes 'Bacq', changed here to the more usual spelling.)

Barbier well-known silk-merchant trading in the Sainte-Opportune quarter in Paris.

Batteux Charles, Abbé Batteux (1713–80), a writer on aesthetics and a member of the Académie Française, was friendly with the Abbé d'Olivet; Diderot was critical of his aesthetic theories.

Bergier Claude François Bergier (1721–84), a lawyer and translator from English. His brother, Nicolas Sylvestre (1718–90), was a theologian who wrote a book (1771) condemning d'Holbach's materialism.

Bernard Samuel Bernard (1651–1739), famous banker of Protestant origins, who made a loan to Louis XIV.

Bertin Louis Auguste Bertin de Blagny, a tax farmer (*fermier général*) and wealthy protector of writers hostile to the philosophes' cause. The break-up of his affair with Mlle Hus was much discussed. He was known to be the protector of Jean-François Rameau.

Bissy Claude-Henri de Bissy, Comte de Thiard, member of the Académie Française, translator of Bolingbroke and Young.

Bouret Étienne Michel Bouret de Silhouette (1710–77), son of a lackey, who became immensely rich. He was treasurer of the King's household, and head of the tax-collecting department. He showed servile obedience to the King and was protector to authors hostile to the party of the philosophes.

Bouvillon Mme Bouvillon is a (very fat) character in Scarron's novel *Le Roman comique* (1657).

Bret Antoine Bret (1717–92), minor playwright, and from 1775 director of *La Gazette de France*, a journal which was hostile to the philosophes.

Briasson Antoine-Claude Briasson (1700–75), one of the booksellers associated with the publication of the *Encyclopédie*.

Brun perhaps the poet Ponce Denis Écouchard Le Brun, known as Le Brun-Pindare (1729–1807), or his brother Jean-Étienne Le Brun de Granville (1718–65).

Buffon Georges-Louis Leclerc, Comte de Buffon (1707–88), the most famous scientist of his day, and author of the *Natural History*; he was a writer whom Diderot greatly admired.

Burigny Jean Lévesque de Burigny (1692–1785), member of the Académie des Inscriptions, author of historical and biographical works, in the circle of Mme Geoffrin; he was also, as Diderot would have been aware, an atheist, who published in 1766 a clandestine critique of Christianity.

Caesar Gaius Julius Caesar (100–44 BC), Roman statesman and military leader.

Caffarelli Gaetano Majorano Caffarelli (1703–83), castrato singer. He performed in Paris in 1753, and the time of the 'Querelle des Bouffons', when he was much applauded by the partisans of Italian music.

Campra André Campra (1660–1744), composer who wrote for the court and originated the genre of the opéra-ballet (*L'Europe galante*, 1697).

Canaye Étienne, Abbé de Canaye (1694–1782), historian and music-lover.

Carmontelle Louis Carrogis, known as Carmontelle (1717–1806), a famous portrait painter, whose portraits include Jean-Philippe Rameau (see frontispiece), and Diderot.

Cicero Marcus Tullius Cicero (106–43 BC), Roman orator, statesman, and writer.

Clairon Mlle Clairon (1723–1802), famous tragic actress, especially in the works of Voltaire. In the *Paradoxe sur le comédien* (*Paradox of the Actor*) Diderot singles her out as the actress whose head perfectly controls her heart, in contrast to Dumesnil, whose performances were more improvised and instinctive.

Corby Nicolas Corby, manager of the Opéra-Comique.

Corneille Pierre Corneille (1606–84), French dramatist of the seventeenth century.

Crébillon the younger Claude-Prosper Jolyot de Crébillon (1707–77), author of libertine novels, and for a time a royal censor, which did not endear him to the philosophes. His reputation as a novelist has been restored in the late twentieth century.

D'Alembert Jean Le Rond D'Alembert (1717–83), a celebrated mathematician, collaborated with Diderot in editing the *Encyclopédie* until 1758, when he withdrew from the project. He was also a close friend (and assiduous correspondent) of Voltaire. He is a central figure in Diderot's *Le Rêve de D'Alembert* (*D'Alembert's Dream*).

Dangeville Anne-Marie Botot, known as la Dangeville (1714–96), highly talented actress who retired from the Comédie-Française in 1763.

Daubenton Louis Daubenton (1716–99), a naturalist and an active collaborator in the *Encyclopédie*.

Dauvergne Antoine Dauvergne (1713–97), opera composer and director of the Opéra. His opéra-comique *Les Troqueurs* (*The Barterers*, 1753) was one of the first to set a French text to music in the Italian style.

David Michel Antoine David the elder, one of the four publishers of the *Encyclopédie*.

Demosthenes the greatest Athenian orator (384–322 BC).

Deschamps Anne-Marie Pagès, known as la Deschamps (*c.*1730–*c.*1775), a dancer at the Opéra who was famous for her dalliances and her extravagance.

Destouches André Cardinal Destouches (1672–1749), pupil of Campra, and remembered as a composer of opera (*Omphale*, 1701).

Diogenes Greek Cynic philosopher of the fourth century BC, supposed to have lived in a barrel; mocked sexual and other conventions.

Dorat Claude-Joseph Dorat (1734–80), a poet of modest talent, hostile to the philosophes; he was praised by Fréron.

Duclos Charles Pinot Duclos (1704–72), a novelist and *moraliste*, and friend of Jean-Jacques Rousseau; he was famously 'frank' and difficult.

Duhamel Henri Louis Duhamel du Monceau (1709–82), a famous writer on agronomy, published *L'Art du charbonnier* (*The Art of the Coalmaker*) in 1760.

Dumesnil Marie-France Marchand, known as la Dumesnil (1714–1803), was a member of the Comédie-Française from 1737, where she was the rival of Mlle Clairon as an interpreter of Voltaire.

Duni Egidio Romualdo Duni (1709–75), composer of opéras-comiques whose success in Paris in the late 1750s revived the 'Querelle des Bouffons' of 1752–3. He was admired by the philosophes.

Egmont the Comtesse d'Egmont (1740–73) was the daughter of the Duc de Richelieu. She was the friend, and perhaps the mistress, of Rulhière, who dedicated several poems to her.

Fenel Jean-Baptiste Fénel (1695–1753), a scholar and member of the Académie des Inscriptions, who wrote a book on the religion of the ancient Gauls.

Ferrein Antoine Ferrein (1693–1769), professor of anatomy and medicine in Paris.

Fontenelle Bernard Le Bovier de Fontenelle (1657–1757), French author and precursor of the philosophes, seen as having provided a model of the didactic dialogue in his *Entretiens sur la pluralité des* mondes (*Conversations on the Plurality of Worlds*, 1686), written in a style which the eighteenth century found somewhat flowery. He also wrote opera libretti.

Foubert a real person, of uncertain identity; possibly a surgeon.

Fréron Élie Catherine Fréron (1718–76), a protégé of the Comtesse de La Marck, and the most celebrated antagonist of the philosophes, whom he attacked in his journal, *L'Année littéraire*. He was involved in endless quarrels with Voltaire, and was a particular enemy of Diderot.

Galiani Ferdinando, Abbé Galiani (1728–87), born in Naples, secretary at the embassy in Paris, 1759–69. Friend of Diderot and of Mme d'Épinay.

Galuppi Baldassare Galuppi (1706–85), composer of operas and of harsichord music.

Geoffrin Mme Marie-Thérèse Geoffrin (1699–1777), who held at her house in the Rue Saint-Honoré an important salon frequented by writers including Fontenelle and D'Alembert.

Greuze Jean-Baptiste Greuze (1725–1805), a painter of portraits and genre scenes, remarkable for their *sensibilité*. In his *Salons*, Diderot expressed enthusiasm for his paintings.

Grotius Hugo De Groot, or Grotius (1583–1645), considered to be the founder of international public law.

Guimard Marie-Madeleine Morelle, known as la Guimard (1743–1816), dancer at the Comédie-Française, then from 1762 at the Opéra. Such was her wealth that she built a private house in Paris containing a theatre for 500 spectators.

Hasse Jean Adolphe Pierre Hasse (1699–1783), known as 'the Saxon', opera composer. In his *Leçons de clavecin*, Diderot considers him to be as famous as Pergolesi.

Helvétius Claude Adrien Helvétius (1715–71), philosophe admired by Diderot; his most important works were *De l'esprit* (1758) and *De l'homme* (1772).

Horace Quintus Horatius Flaccus (65–8 BC), Latin poet in the reign of Augustus, author of *Epistles*, *Satires*, and *Odes*. Familiar in eighteenth-century Europe as one of the best-known and most-loved lyric poets of antiquity. See Introduction for his influence on Diderot's two *Satires*.

Hus Adélaïde Louise Pauline Hus (1734–1805), actress at the Comédie-Française, where she was somewhat eclipsed by Mlle Clairon. She encouraged the performance in that theatre of Palissot's satirical *Les Philosophes*, so was seen as antagonistic to the philosophes' cause.

Javillier Jacques Javillier-Létang, a dancer at the Opéra and dancing master to the King, and a well-known figure in the 1760s.

Jommelli Nicolò Jommelli (1714–74), a prolific composer of operas and sacred music; his *Lamentations* were performed at the Concert spirituel in 1751.

La Bruyère Jean de La Bruyère (1645–96), a writer remembered for *Les Caractères* (*The Characters*, 1688); though seen as a French 'classical' writer, he is in many ways a precursor of the philosophes.

Laïs Greek courtesan.

La Marck, Mme de Marie Anne Françoise de Noailles, Comtesse de La Marck, the protector of Palissot. Not known as a beauty, she became famously devout.

La Morlière Jacques Rochette, chevalier de La Morlière (1701–85), novelist and author of some poor plays; a boisterous character who attracted and enjoyed scandal.

La Motte Antoine Houdar de La Motte (1672–1731), a 'Modern' whose writings include many opera libretti (notably for Dauvergne, Destouches, and Campra).

La Porte the Abbé Joseph de La Porte (1718–79), a collaborator of Fréron who went on to found a rival journal, *L'Observateur littéraire* (1758–61).

Le Blanc Jean-Bernard, Abbé Le Blanc (1707–81), a translator of works from English; a protégé of Mme de Pompadour, he nonetheless failed to win entry to the Académie Française; he was hostile to the philosophes.

Legal A Breton gentleman and famous chess-player who gave lessons to Philidor.

Lemierre Marie-Jeanne Lemierre (1733–86), a singer who made her debut at the Opéra in 1750; she was the mistress of the Prince de Conti, and married the singer Larrivée in 1762.

Leo Leonardo Leo (1694–1746), Neapolitan composer of operas and sacred music, disciple of Scarlatti.

Locatelli Pietro Locatelli (1695–1764), from Bergamo, a composer of challenging pieces for the violin, and a virtuoso player himself.

Lully Jean-Baptiste Lully (1632–87), born in Florence, the most prominent composer at the court of Louis XIV. By the mid-eighteenth century his music seemed too simple in comparison with that of Rameau.

Marcus Aurelius Roman emperor (AD 161–80) and author of the *Meditations*.

Marivaux Pierre Carlet de Chamblain de Marivaux (1688–1763), novelist, journalist, and prolific dramatist; but the philosophes viewed him as a 'Modern' who lacked the higher taste.

Mayot A chess-player, otherwise unknown.

Metastasio Pierre Bonaventure Trapassi, known as Metastasio (1698–1782), celebrated poet and librettist. He was innovative in his manner of conceiving the relationship between music and text, and his opera libretti were set by composers including Gluck and Mozart.

Moette Pierre Moette, manager of the Opéra-Comique.

Molière Jean-Baptiste Poquelin, known as Molière (1622–73), the greatest French comic playwright, already regarded as a 'classic' in the eighteenth century.

Montamy Didier François d'Arclais de Montamy (1704–65), close to d'Holbach and Diderot, tried in vain to discover the formula for making Chinese porcelain; the Comte de Lauraguais claimed to have discovered this already in 1764.

Monsauge Denis Philippe Thiroux de Montsauge, remembered for having supported the play *Les Philosophes* which satirized the philosophes. Like Villemorien, he was a son-in-law of Bouret, with whom he was associated.

Montbron Louis-Charles Fougeret de Montbron, author of minor works, including a pornographic novel and a burlesque verse travesty of Voltaire's *La Henriade*. He was a famous eccentric.

Montesquieu Charles de Secondat, Baron de Montesquieu (1689–1755), philosophe, author of the *Lettres persanes* (*Persian Letters*, 1721), the first major satire of the French Enlightenment, and of *De l'esprit des lois* (*The Spirit of the Laws*, 1748), a major work of political philosophy.

Mouret Jean-Joseph Mouret (1682–1738), composer and rival of Rameau, prominent during the Regency.

Muret Marc Antoine Muret (1526–85), humanist and philologist.

Naigeon Jacques-André Naigeon (1738–1810), a close friend and collaborator of Diderot, who mocked the intransigence of his militantly anticlerical views. He was responsible for the first collected edition of Diderot's works, published in fifteen volumes (1798).

Noël Père Noël, a Benedictine from Rheims, sold optical instruments and supplied the royal household.

Noverre Jean Georges Noverre (1737–1810), ballet master at the Opéra-Comique, 1753–6, and author of *Lettres sur la danse et sur les ballets*.

Olivet Pierre-Joseph Thoulier, Abbé d'Olivet (1682–1768), grammarian and member of the Académie Française, hostile to the philosophes. Diderot thought him a dangerous hypocrite.

Palissot Charles Palissot de Montenoy (1730–1814), a writer who mocked the philosophes, and Diderot in particular, most notably in his successful play *Les Philosophes* (1760).

Pellegrin Abbé Simon Joseph Pellegrin (1663–1745), author of opera libretti, including that of *Hippolyte et Aricie* for Rameau.

Pericles great Athenian statesman (*c.* 495–429 BC).

Pergolesi Giovanni Battista Pergolesi (1710–36), composer remembered for *La Serva padrona* (1733) and the *Stabat Mater* (1736). When his work was performed in Paris in the early 1750s it became emblematic of the 'new' Italian style.

Philidor François-André Danican Philidor (1726–95) was equally famous as a chess-player and as a composer; his operas include *Le Maréchal-Ferrant* and *Ernelinde*. He probably taught harmony to Diderot's daughter, Angélique.

Phryne Greek courtesan of the fourth century BC.

Piron Alexis Piron (1689–1773), a playwright and poet, no favourite of the philosophes.

Poinsinet Antoine Henri Poinsinet (1735–69), an absurd bohemian Grub Street writer, who aped Palissot in his hostility to the philosophes. His cousin Louis Poinsinet de Sivry (1733–1804) was a translator who also wrote plays mocking the philosophes.

Préville Pierre-Louis Dubus, known as Préville (1721–99), a Comédie-Française actor famous for his skills at pantomime. He scored a great success in Boursault's *Le Mercure galant* when it was revived in 1753; he would later play Figaro in Beaumarchais's *The Barber of Seville*.

Pufendorf Samuel Pufendorf (1632–94), historian and jurist. He and Grotius (whose disciple he was) were formative influences on Enlightenment legal and political thought.

Quinault Philippe Quinault (1635–88), author of tragedies, but best remembered as Lully's' librettist.

Rabelais François Rabelais (d. 1553), French humanist and author of comic fictions. Diderot admired his works, which were generally dismissed as obscene in the eighteenth century.

Racine Jean Racine (1639–99), the great seventeenth-century tragedian, whose reputation in the eighteenth century stood very high. Diderot, no poet and no tragedian himself, was a great admirer.

Rameau Jean-Philippe Rameau (1683–1764), pre-eminent French composer of the eighteenth century. His nephew, Jean-François, provides the model for 'Him'.

Rémond de Saint-Mard Toussaint Rémond de Saint-Mard (1682–1757), minor author who wrote on, among other things, aesthetics and opera.

Glossary of Names

Réaumur René Antoine Ferchault de Réaumur (1683–1757), eminent entomologist and physician, and author of *Mémoires pour servir à l'histoire des insectes* (1734–42). Diderot criticized his work for being overly methodical; Réaumur accused the encyclopedists of plagiarizing him.

Rey the Abbé Rey, perhaps the author of *Considérations philosophiques sur le christianisme* (*Philosophical Observations on Christianity*, 1785).

Rinaldo da Capua Rinaldo da Capua (1717–65), Neapolitan composer whose works were performed in Paris in 1752–3.

Robbé Robbé de Beauveset (1725–94), an utterly mediocre poet, remembered, if at all, for a poem on smallpox.

Rousseau Jean-Jacques Rousseau (1712–78), one of the most influential and controversial writers of the French Enlightenment; his emphasis on nature and feeling set him apart from the other philosophes, with whom he was on uneasy terms.

Rulhière Claude de Rulhière (1734–91), French diplomat, historian, and poet.

Socrates Athenian philosopher of the fifth century BC, teacher of Plato, and especially remembered for his 'stoic' death when he drank hemlock (a scene which David would paint). He was a constant model for Diderot, who translated the *Apology* when in prison at Vincennes.

Stentor a character in Homer's *Iliad* whose powerful voice equalled that of fifty men in unison.

Tartini Giuseppe Tartini (1692–1770), composer and virtuoso violinist.

Tencin Claudine Alexandrine Guérin de Tencin (1685–1749), a successful novelist and the hostess of an important salon which assembled such writers as Fontenelle, Montesquieu, Marivaux, and Helvétius. She was the mother of D'Alembert, whom she abandoned as a baby on the steps of a church. Her brother Pierre Guérin, Cardinal de Tencin (1679–1758), was protected by Fleury. His secretary was the Abbé Trublet.

Terradeglias Dominique Michel Barnabé Terradeglias (or Terradellas) (1713–51), Spanish composer of operas and sacred music, working in Rome.

Theophrastus Greek classical author of the fourth century BC, remembered for his *Characters*, a collection of sketches depicting character types. Translated and imitated by La Bruyère in the seventeenth century.

Thierry François Thierry (or Thiéry) (1718–92), a doctor in the Faculty of Paris from 1750, who attended on the King.

Thomas Antoine Léonard Thomas (1732–85), member of the Académie Française, famous for his academic 'éloges'. Diderot was an admirer of his belief that ethics should be based on natural principles.

Traetta Tommaso Traetta (or Trajetta) (1727–79), Italian opera composer attached to various European courts.

Trublet the Abbé Nicolas Joseph Charles Trublet (1697–1770), a writer and defender of the 'Moderns', who was at one time secretary to Cardinal de Tencin.

Turenne Henri de la Tour d'Auvergne, Vicomte de Turenne (1611–75), Marshal of France and outstanding general in Louis XIV's early campaigns.

Vauban Sébastien Le Prestre, Seigneur de Vauban (1633–1707), celebrated military strategist in the reign of Louis XIV.

Villemorien Philippe Charles Le Gendre de Villemorien, a tax farmer (*fermier général*) and *administrateur général* of the post office; son-in-law of Bouret.

Vinci Leonardo Vinci (1696–1730), opera composer, succeeded Scarlatti as director of the royal chapel at Naples.

Voltaire François-Marie Arouet, known as Voltaire (1694–1778), the most celebrated philosophe of the French Enlightenment; in religious matters he was a deist, and less radical than Diderot, who admired the older man while being wary of him.